A Selfless Sacrifice

PAUL CUDE

CONTENTS

PROLOGUE

Twenty thousand years ago the planet only vaguely resembled what it is today. The geography, climate and politics were very different, with the height of the humans' talent expressing itself in rudimentary cave paintings and the occasional grunt here and there, making their mark as only the odd snack or two for something much larger. In the bigger picture, they as a species were barely noticeable as the world continued to be dominated by the most mighty apex predator of them all... DRAGONS!

A SELFLESS SACRIFICE

Glancing back over his shoulder, the ache in the pit of his stomach trebled when he realised the trouble he was in. What looked like another fifty adversaries had popped up on the horizon in every conceivable shade, rapidly closing in on his position, belching fireballs, baring their razor sharp teeth, all offering angry snarls and withering looks, desperate to get their claws and talons into him.

Banking back away from them, soaking up the sun through the crystal clear blue sky, reflecting on a brief moment of perfection, with the rays warming his radiant cranberry coloured wings, the briefest tinge of fear tickled the innards of his mind.

'Will this be it?' he thought wistfully. 'Have I finally bitten off more than I can chew?' That would be ironic given his love of trying to eat livestock whole. About to use his considerable will to push the negativity aside, the need to do so vanished as an image materialised inside his head, taking over everything. Instantly he recognised the massive grey and desolate rocky outcrop on the far side of the forest, the one that must have extended out beyond a thousand wingspans, the entrance the craggy overhang often used as an emergency shelter in case of unexpected electrical storms, something no dragon ever wishes to find his or herself trapped in.

Pulled into the picture in his mind, a will he immediately recognised flooded his body, urging him with everything it had to fly into the darkened entrance below the menacing outcrop. Swallowing nervously as he cut through the warm summer air, the wind tickling the scales on the underside of his regal belly and the length of his humungous tail as he pumped his powerful wings, the realisation of just how badly outnumbered he was left him in no doubt about his options. And so in a leap of faith, one not totally unfamiliar to him, he gracefully plunged down towards the top of the lush green canopy below in the hope that just maybe he could buy himself enough time to reach the proffered destination.

Landing with an almighty THUD at the opposite end of the forest on the bleak, rocky outcrop, For'son's legs nearly crumpled under the massive strain of his gigantic prehistoric body, the gleaming white talons that marked him out as extraordinary ripping the harsh ground apart. Shaking off the day's fatigue, the sense of urgency that had previously threatened to overwhelm him came back with a vengeance, concern for his friend rearing its ugly head like a yeti in a snowstorm. With no time to lose, and knowing that he had to get this just right, the bright intelligent spark within him started running calculations on where he needed to begin, the depth to which he had to go, and just how long it would take him to chew up the material above the outcrop with his talons alone. Almost immediately a conclusion was reached. And it wasn't a positive one. The distance was too far, by quite some way, meaning that he'd never do it in time. Well, not using only his physical prowess. And so there was only ever going to be one solution... MAGIC!

Searching the vast repository of mantras (that's a spell, hex or enchantment to you or me) in his brain, faster than a present day supercomputer could beat a novice at a game of chess, the valiant dragon hero selected something suitable that he hoped would do the trick. Scaled eyelids falling silently shut he closed off his mind, applied his indomitable will, and inside his head, whispered the words,

"Proferet lava pedes."

Roughly translating as 'bring forth lava feet', a deep sense of satisfaction washed over him as a tentative heat blossomed out from around the end of his legs. Arching his prodigious neck, unable to do anything but use his giant monster of a head to look down, even though he'd done it once before, the sight of his previously bright, white talons now swirling in shades of orange, red and yellow, steam rising off them still startled him somewhat. That is until the tiniest nip at the back of his mind served as a reminder of what he was supposed to be doing. With minute adjustments to the complicated equations that he'd already formulated, immediately he picked two spots, planted his talons firmly down and watched wide-eyed as they sunk into the thick grey stone, melting it instantly. Straining the muscles in his enormous legs, almost to breaking point, while keeping what were effectively his toes buried into the rock, he thrust down his wings with all the force he could muster and started to propel himself forward. Molten magma in the exact shape of his previously white talons carved through the thick, untouched stone on top of the overhang in much the same way a hot knife would slice its way through butter. With every flap of his wings, he moved faster, ever closer to the forest his friend was now flying over.

Not needing to even look back over his shoulders, he knew without a doubt that they were gaining on him, his finely honed magical senses feeling their every movement, aware of just how many there were and how they were closing in all around. Staving off the panic of getting caught, dodging the odd far ranged fireball and explosive magical attack here, and the occasional mental assault there, he knew without a doubt that something had to change for him to be able to make it as far as the dark and mysterious entrance. What to do though, that was the question.

It was then that the feeling of leaves from the tree canopy prickled the sensitive scales on his underbelly, forcing him up a metre or so. Annoyed at not paying enough attention to his flying, thoughts focused on the trees themselves, it was then that the light bulb moment struck, something that he was immediately grateful for.

Pushing aside thoughts of just how many pursuers there were, instinctively he dipped into his somewhat depleted well of mana, or his magical reserves as he liked to think of it, and stretching out with his mind, set out to find something which might at least buy him a little leeway.

Sensing the upper canopy, the leaves of the trees violently rustling in his wake, caterpillars clinging on for dear life, birds scattering into the air, the supernatural within him pushed on, brushing against the rough brown bark of the trunks all lined up like soldiers on parade.

'Almost there,' he thought, knowing how close he now was.

Giving it all he had, lush green grass swam into view, thinly bent blades looking like giant skyscrapers as his mind nose-dived past them, as well as decomposing leaves and animal droppings, into the densely packed, rich brown earth. Ignoring sleeping earthworms and bustling ants, still the power within him pushed on, until that is, it found exactly what it was looking for... a confusing tangle of life. That's right, he'd reached the root system of all the trees in the forest below, the writhing mass of tendrils twisting and turning beneath the ground, drawing nutrients and surprisingly, to him anyway, communicating with one another. Momentarily this made him reconsider what he had planned, unfortunately though, there was no going back and his need was great. They'd be on him in a matter of moments. If he didn't act now, he'd be a goner for sure. Apologising to the forest as a whole, well... in his mind at least, he gripped the roots of one of the massive pine trees and applying some of his will, with just a thought, ripped the monstrous plant out of the ground, propelling it skyward like the launch of a rocket.

BOOM! In one swift stroke it shot right up through the underbelly of the closest dragon to him, the tip bursting through the dull yellow coloured scales of his back, instantly rendering him dead. With no time to watch

PAUL CUDE

the skewered monster spiral clumsily to the ground, his intellect still firmly focused on the job, he gripped yet another set of roots, sending that pine rocketing skyward, and then the next and the next until, in his wake, all you could see was a forest of trees, all hurtling through the air, pounding prehistoric bodies, piercing wings, shattering bones, destroying skulls. He lost count after sending twenty pines shooting up into the cool, fresh air, each of them hitting their mark, decimating nearly half of the force chasing after him, causing those remaining to fall back in fear.

Returning all his concentration to flying, once again brushing dangerously close to the top of the trees that he'd just used as weapons, head spinning from the over use of his magic, the dragon king, for that's who he was, streaked ever onward towards the overhang that he was being guided towards at quite a dizzying rate, temporarily able to breathe a sigh of relief.

Reaching the end of the rocky overhang, able to look out over the sea of green that was the forest below him, For'son turned back to admire his work. Looking like a railway line without sleepers embedded into the plateau itself, the two parallel lines disappeared off into the distance as far as the eye could see, substantially weakening the structure, something that he hoped would play right into their hands.

'And not a moment too soon,' he mused, spotting his friend far off in the distance, against the background of brilliant green trees shooting up into the air.

'Ohhh... nice. I like that one. I must remember to get you to teach it to me when this is all over,' he thought.

Lingering for but a moment longer, admiring everything about his friend, the dragon king and one of the fiercest warriors on the planet, For'son's sense of the moment finally kicked in. Satisfied with his work up until

6

now, he swung down over the far side of the outcrop, a perfect place to hide from the onrushing dragons, and still using his molten magma talons, carved himself some footholds so that he could hang in place without being seen. Safely hidden, once again he reached out in search of his comrade's psyche and, upon finding it, showered it with the dark and lonely image of the sheltered entrance, hoping he would take the hint.

There it was again, a perfect depiction of the cold and secluded entrance to the rock-strewn overhang blossoming to life right before his very eyes as he rallied against the pull of gravity on his huge, scaled, prehistoric body.

'This had better work,' thought the king, knowing that if it didn't, there'd be no one around to answer for it. And so slightly reluctantly, he hissed through the air and closing fast, headed for the darkness that offered itself up, wondering where exactly his friend was in all of this, all the time aware that his attackers were gaining on him, their confidence increased as the forest transformed into rock.

Clinging silently onto the shadowy stone face at the rear of the outcrop, all his magical senses effectively powered down, he didn't need them to tell that his ploy had worked and his friend had darted at speed into the gap just big enough to support him beneath the overhang, his adversaries following hot on his tail one by one, as that's the only way they could be accommodated inside the huge structure, the roar of their bodies and the wind in their wake assaulting not only his ears but the rest of him as well.

Waiting until the last of them sped off into the dark, For'son leapt off the sheer wall that he clung to, and with one flap of his mighty wings, came down next to the parallel lines that he'd already cut on top of the outcrop.

Knowing exactly how deep they were and sure of just how much they'd weakened the structure, the crafty dragon knew that it was now or never if he wanted to catch up with the rest of them. Bounding into the air, he took off only a metre or so above the rock, throwing up dust, pebbles and small boulders in his wake. Taking a deep breath, inundating it with that special feeling at the pit of his stomach, he exhaled as he sped along, blowing out a constant stream of fire in front of him, directly down at the lines he'd already cut. And that was enough. Enough for what, I hear you ask... Enough to collapse the overhang in on itself, its main support already weakened by his lava talons earlier.

Pouring on as much speed as he could, focused solely on catching up with the murderous horde pursuing his friend and king, For'son cut through the very atoms of the air itself in his attempt to gain as much velocity as possible, the powerful muscles in his wings burning with agonising pain. Soaring along, roaring a crackling cone of orange, yellow, red and blue flame into the stony ground beneath him, a thunderous growl of rock collapsing in on itself got ever louder, bombarding the ears of the flying fortress For'son. But that was nothing to what was happening beneath him.

As soon as he accelerated forward into the darkness, instinct kicked in, and he switched over to what he liked to think of as his 'hunting at night vision', something we would refer to now as infrared. Bringing to life the tightly fitting, narrow tunnel that he found himself trapped in, it was all he could do to fight back the claustrophobia that threatened to overwhelm him. After all, dragons like clear, open blue skies on days very much like today, with the sun beating down on their wings, basking their whole bodies, heating them up to their full potential. Stuck in a confined, dark space was far from ideal, and just when he thought it couldn't get any worse, the sound of rock crashing against rock from somewhere behind him in the distance echoed off the walls.

'Damn,' he reflected, now seeing what his friend was up to, 'you and I really are going to have to have a chat about the recklessness of your schemes and whether or not it should be me being used as the bait.'

With little choice but to increase the pace with which he was travelling, the tips of his wings already brushing against the rough stone walls on either side of him, the king cursed his luck, tried to apply as much power as he dared, attempted to zero in on the distant exit and concentrated on today's bigger picture, well aware that victory was still a real possibility.

Trapped, fearful of being in a darkened, confined space with absolutely no possibility of turning around, those dragons that had followed their prey into what they thought was a little hidey hole were only just realising the magnitude of their mistake as the stone ceiling started to collapse from somewhere back at the rear. Powered by sheer terror and the thought of dying in somewhere like this, those that remained alive gave everything they had in an effort to outrun the inevitable.

Sweating profusely, throat red raw from the constant stream of fire he continued to focus on the rock below him, For'son, unencumbered by being out in the open, moved faster than any of those underground, easily catching his friend's pursuers, bringing thousands of tonnes of rock down on them in just a few seconds. Only a matter of a hundred or so wingspans up ahead, he could feel the king in the lead, using all his knowledge of flight to stay out in front, managing for now to outrun the crushing wave of debris that he was bringing down on the lot of them. Over two thirds of the way through the entire length of the structure, it was only then, sensing the fear and sudden surge in speed by those chasing down his pal, that the audacious dragon above ground realised his mistake. He hadn't bargained for their adversaries, in their terror induced states, ploughing everything they had into the speed they needed to catch up with their prey. With that sudden surge, there and then he knew that catching them up to finish them off, as he'd planned, just wouldn't be possible. Improvising on the hoof, still zipping along at an alarmingly quick rate, For'son, not really wanting to distract the king from his already perilous state, figured that he now had no choice. Opening up his mind, he instantly found that of his friend, and ignoring all the usual formalities, spoke quickly and calmly.

"I'm sorry, I've misjudged. I've taken out most of them, but the rest, maybe ten or so, will be upon you before I can finish them off. You'll have to try and collapse it from the inside. Good luck!"

'BRILLIANT!' thought the king, his mind already working overtime, dodging out of the way of the occasional fissure here, the odd bump in the ground there, his enhanced vision only picking them up once he was upon them, that's how fast he was travelling. Just when it seemed impossible for things to get any worse, his nagging sense of danger kicked in and he got a sense of precisely how close the enemy immediately behind him had gotten. CLOSE, that was for sure, almost within biting range. Not able to take his concentration or vision away from what he was doing because of the inevitable crash that would ensue, he had only one thought about what to do to extricate himself from this, the most impossible of positions, with even that being as daft as a brush. Offering up the briefest of prayers to the dragon king god, Idra, somewhere deep within his mind, he shook his head and in one all encompassing, startling move, rolled axially so that he became inverted, his belly now facing the ceiling instead of the floor. Caught by surprise, the malevolent beast behind him lost ground immediately, shocked at why a dragon would do that. Any moment now though, he was about to find out. Arching his long, taut scaled neck back as far as it would go so that he could just about see the way ahead still, the king, one of the finest warrior dragons to ever grace the planet, sucked in his breath and using just an inkling of his magical birthright, commanded the fire within him to come to life. Immediately it did, responding to his familiar touch, the blistering heat and flame racing up his oesophagus, into his mouth, the warmth tickling his sharp jagged teeth as he opened wide. In one large and loud belch, he spat the giant fireball out in front of him, which given his precarious position, meant straight into the ceiling of the tunnel he was flying upside down along. And just out of the corner of one eye, he got to see the fearful final look on his pursuer's face, right before a mountainous amount of rock came descending down between the two of them.

Briefly delighted, he immediately righted a wrong and inverted back, zigzagging around two giant boulders unexpectedly jutting out from beyond one of the darkened walls. Exhaling sharply, a pinprick of light up ahead suddenly swam into view. Swapping back to his normal vision and with nothing else chasing him, elegantly he glided towards the onrushing exit, looking forward to the sun once again baking his huge scaled body. Making the most of his momentum, the king twisted slightly to line himself up with the odd shaped hole at the end of the outcrop, and then, like a phoenix flying out of the flames, shot out of the darkness and into the crystal clear, cloudless blue sky. Stretching out every sinew in his wings as he effortlessly looped the loop, the warm rush of air caressing every single scale on the outside of his prehistoric body. It wasn't long before his friend joined him in the air above the end of the rocky overhang.

"Yet another stunning plan," ventured the king

sarcastically.

"Ahhh... what are you moaning about? It worked didn't it?"

"Hmmm... I suppose."

"And just what else was I going to do at such short notice? You probably need to take better care and not get caught up in those kind of situations," declared For'son, hot on his friend's tail, tumbling and rolling, jinking this way and that, both of them trying to outfly the other in, of course, the most friendly way possible.

"You always have an answer for everything, don't you?" observed the dragon monarch, tiny flecks of sizzling orange flame flicking out of his huge, scaled nostrils.

"What can I say?" replied his friend. "It's a gift, and one I utilise to its utmost."

Abruptly the light of the day faded, leaving them both shrouded in darkness and shadow, which was odd because dusk was a long way off and there hadn't been one single cloud in the sky. As one, they turned to face where they knew the sun was, both hovering in the air.

Horrific blackness filled the sky, blocking out most of what remained of the sunlight, sending a terrifying chill up both friends' spines as they tried in vain to make out exactly what had happened.

"Uhh... Majesty, I think it might be time to leave," whispered For'son, not normally nearly so cautious.

"I just want to see what..."

"Uhh... Majesty, we really have to go."

"I just want to know what..."

"Dragons sire, and a lot of them."

"Don't be ridiculous For'son, there's no way in hell that it could be..."

"You see?"

"Oh..."

Simultaneously the king and his friend wheeled around and using the full force of their mighty wings, started hightailing it off in the opposite direction to the dark force of monstrous winged beasts that had, through sheer numbers, blocked out the light from the sun.

"Make for the swamp," shouted For'son across the barrage of noise from the wind whipping their faces.

"Another one of your excellent plans?" enquired the king sceptically.

"Something like that."

Not daring to look back over their shoulders, both friends flew for all they were worth. After five or six minutes the terrain beneath them started to visibly change, the jagged grey rocks with the occasional pine sticking out faded away, replaced by lush wet grass and thick brown waterways, all noticeably flat, with absolutely no cover or defensive hidey holes anywhere.

Tired and now thirsty, the king was the first one of them to pause and look back, albeit only momentarily, hovering casually above the fetid swamp.

"There must be hundreds of them, For'son. What the hell are we going to do?"

"Follow me sire, and have a little faith," his friend suggested with a smile and a wink.

That was when the monarch knew they had a fighting chance.

Kicking the king playfully in the thigh with one of his huge feet, his talons retracted, the lava magic long since having disappeared, For'son arched his neck, pinwheeled around and pumping his powerful wings ferociously, once again headed away at speed from the oncoming pack of death dealing monsters all journeying in their direction. Smiling at the audacity of his friend, the sovereign, buoyed by the thought of whatever was up For'son's magical sleeve, turned and followed in his wake, exerting a great deal of energy in an effort to catch him up.

'Ohhh,'" he thought, 'this is going to be good.'

Barely a wing width apart, five hundred or so dragons

in all shapes, colours and sizes, led by their ruthless, heartless and callous leader, Prtzillines, swept through the air high above the ground, the sun blazing down on their backs, heating their scales and the desire within them to follow the orders that had been laid out in front of them by their despotic leader. Kill those outsiders that would try and interfere in their sadistic way of life. Leave no stone unturned in doing exactly that, no matter what it meant and no matter how far they had to travel. Send a message to the rest of the world, that under no circumstances were they to be trifled with. And so with murder on their mind, they closed in on their prey, their timeworn instincts to kill and maim in order to protect their own, bubbling to the surface, each ready to do what it took to take down these interfering usurpers.

The muscles in their tails and wings aching like a weightlifter's back, darting out briefly in front of his friend For'son unexpectedly pulled up, and then dropped to the marshy ground, landing with a splash amongst the various shades of long, wet, green grass and in doing so turned back to face the raging horde rampaging through the air after them. Tiny effervescing bubbles wriggled their way to the surface as far as the eye could see giving off a fetid aroma of... what? An underground natural phenomenon specific only to that area or the waft of dead animals being brutally digested by something prehistoric? Had they thought about it, their enemy might just have recognised the singularity, but of course they didn't.

Following his lead, the king dropped down beside him, the cold muddy water splattering half way up his thighs as he did so.

"Perhaps now would be a good time to fill me in?" asked the monarch, fully expecting the details to be forthcoming.

Boy was he disappointed.

"When they get here, speak to their leader, Prtzillines. Make it clear that you'll accept their surrender and that the citizens and the land as a whole will benefit greatly by living under your banner."

"And..."

"And that's it," he replied.

"You do realise that they're going to kill us, in the most despicable way possible," added the sovereign.

"Ahhh, well you never really know. Perhaps your regal reasoning will leave them dumbfounded, confused but also impressed."

The look on the king's face was absolutely priceless at his friend's clowning about in the circumstances they now found themselves.

"I bet you wish you hadn't cancelled my order for reinforcements right about now," admonished For'son, half jokingly.

The ruler did... big time!

"As always, you were right, but a fat lot of good that's going to do us now, unless of course you can magic them out of thin air from an entire continent away."

"I wish that were the case, but not so I'm afraid."

"Oh good."

"Anyhow, here they come. Good luck!" wished his friend, taking one step back.

'What in the hell have I got myself caught up in this time?' he wondered, puffing out his dark red belly as far as it would go in the hope that it would make him look somehow majestic and unappetising.

Almost immediately they were upon them, at first the whole force circling through the air above, making sure there was nowhere for the two of them to go, and then following the example of their prey they landed, all five hundred of them, in a gigantic circle, leaving a large open space of about twenty wingspans between them and their quarry.

Swallowing nervously, facing the despicable and

murderous leader that he'd only recently met diplomatically in an effort to once and for all reunite his entire land for the good of the world as a whole, the king attempted to do as his friend had asked, once again trusting For'son to deliver. Not once had he ever previously let him down. There is however, always a first time for everything.

"Well... if it isn't, now... how did you so shamelessly put it on your visit? Ahh... that's it, the king of the free world. If it isn't the king of the free world, lost, alone and interfering in what is most definitely our part of it."

Swallowing nervously, able to look out, because of his specially shaped eyes, at a great deal of them, probably more than three hundred, all eyeing him up for some spectacular death no doubt, the monarch of most of the new world, something he'd spent decades trying to reunite, remembered his friend's words and ploughed on despite the tangible danger that was everywhere around him and the all encompassing fear that surged through his veins. Moments like this were what it was all about.

"Prtzillines, it's so good to see you again. Out hunting with your friends? I'd rather hoped you'd taken on board what I said about the bipeds."

"Oh... we're out hunting, and while I totally disagree about your stance on the bipeds, you don't have to worry about that today, they're not the prey we're looking for."

A huge round of chortling echoed throughout the concentric circle of desperate, deadly beings surrounding the king and For'son at this, all kowtowing to their leader's supposed charm and wit, each knowing what the repercussions would be if they didn't join in.

"I see," mused the monarch, much to the amusement of those all around.

"Seeking to covertly infiltrate our lands in order to persuade my subjects to go behind my back and support you seems to have backfired. I bet you wish now that you hadn't gone against my will, and that you'd just left us alone. Those under me know no rule of law except mine. Whether you like it or not is neither here nor there. I've been doing this for an awfully long time, and will continue to do so until the day I die, something that will be centuries from now. But enough talking. I'm sick and tired of everything that's gone on here today, and although it gives me no pleasure at all," he said, a sickly grin forming across the scales of his prehistoric face, "it's time to show you how trespassers are treated away from your precious domain."

With the time for the most one-sided fight in history arriving with something of a whimper, the dragon domain king tried to stick to the plot.

"I'll graciously accept your surrender, you should know," he piped up to a chorus of laughter and cheers from the surrounding malevolent monsters.

"Is that so?" replied Prtzillines, starting to lose his temper.

"It is," answered For'son's best friend. "And I'll also guarantee a kinder, grander life, less under threat for all of the beings you claim to command. We'll build dwellings underground and on the surface. They'll be able to travel freely wherever they want, join and interact with different communities, exchanging ideas and magic with likeminded individuals. Roles in local government, and even the dragon council itself would all be possibilities. Tell me that's not an upgrade on what they've already got? Sustainable resources for food, shelter from the harsh cold of the winter, with enough goodwill to go around. And all you have to do is step down and live the rest of your life in comfort and relative obscurity. That's not too much to ask, is it?"

This time there was no laughter, no cheering... nothing except a cold harsh silence, only pierced by the occasional bubble bursting on the surface of the water they all stood in.

"And," added the head of state, "if you can't do it for

yourself, do it for all those surrounding you and their families. Think of their struggle and wellbeing and just how much this might improve THEIR lives."

'Ohhh,' thought For'son from ever so slightly behind his friend. 'I like that, I really do. I wonder if he'll take the bait?'

Stretching out his dark green powerful wings in the blink of an eye and turning ever so slightly, knocking those around him into the water at his feet, most landing with an ungainly splash, the deranged and fearless leader of this land huffed out a few breaths of extraordinary bright and hot fire from between his humungous jaws in an effort to intimidate his troops close by, as he conjured up the words he needed to put these invaders in their place.

"You think that uniting all of those other lands under one banner gives you the right to come storming back in here after not getting the answer that you wanted just a short while ago. Let me tell you now... it doesn't! These male and female dragons are mine to command and always will be. I don't care about your brave new life, or how much better off they'll be. I only care about running my land as I see fit, and nobody, and I mean, nobody, interferes in that. With that in mind, I'm about to show you the result of meddling and just what happens to any being that disobeys me."

'Bluster, yes,' thought the king, 'but something he could probably follow through on. Come on For'son, I think we've played games for long enough. Show your hand, and let's be done with all of this.'

About to give the command for one all out attack, for his troops to rip into the two stray dragons out some way in front of them, Prtzillines was very rudely interrupted.

"Tell me, have you always been so ignorant and arrogant?" asked For'son, stepping up next to his comrade, much more full of confidence than he had any right to be.

Murderous anger writhing in the deathly dark pupils of his giant, beastly eyes, the vile and disgraceful leader of this land didn't miss a beat with his reply.

"I'd have thought your last words would have been something more memorable and wise," he growled, instigating more howling and laughter, the dragons around him this time beating their wings in fury and anticipation of what was to come.

To their utter surprise, For'son stood there, heavily outnumbered and just... puffed out his bright, crystal blue chest in a gesture of defiance.

Beside him, the king gulped.

"Get ready," mouthed Prtzillines, silently.

And then, it happened, utterly without warning.

The occasional bubbles across the swamp, well, their part of it anyway, increased by a thousand fold, gurgling and effervescing, belching and squelching. On their own not so much a cause for alarm, but in tandem with five thousand dragons rising up out of the watery gloom and into the ferocious sunlight, in a concentric circle not only between their king and the dark enemy force but all around the outer circumference of those that would do their monarch harm. An impressive sight to be sure, with the odds now changing significantly in favour of For'son and his friend.

As mighty prehistoric beasts shook off the water, mud and filth they'd been hiding in, the enemy force trapped between their two rings of fighters looked on in absolute fear, something they'd previously only experienced at the hands of their leader, the one who now stood out gazing across through a small gap in the enemy lines that allowed a view of For'son and the king, looking perplexed at how events had unfolded over the last few seconds. From the expression emblazoned onto his monstrous, dinosaur-like face, things could go either way.

"Y... y... y... you cheated!" he exclaimed. "Y... y... y... you lied and deceived!"

"Not at all," responded the king, relieved at part of his army turning up without his knowledge, thankful that his friend had, not for the first time, disobeyed a direct order and gone with what he thought best.

"We'd always hoped to do this the easy way, to convince you to step down and live the rest of your life in relative luxury, affording the dragons under you a fresh start and a new way of life without fear and threats, without the abuse and suffering that has become your trademark. However, you've chosen not to follow this course of action, endangering your subjects, but also the rest of the planet. And I'm afraid I just can't allow that to happen. And so I'll say this now, in front of every being here. At this exact moment, YOU HAVE A CHOICE! You can follow your monstrous leader's order which will no doubt be to charge and attempt to take at least ME out, or you can surrender to us of your own free will, return to your families and grasp the chance of a new, free life with both hands. I'm not going to lie to you... it won't be easy, at least not to start with, but what we're doing across the planet will build a platform for every dragon to thrive, and a superior life in the future for all our offspring. The choice is of course... YOURS! But a better offer will not come again in your lifetime, which, given your leader's next order, could well be measured in only a matter of seconds."

And there he finished, furtively eyeing his adversary and those all around him, waiting to see how the next few moments would play out, pretty sure he already knew.

Stuck in his ways, used to his orders being obeyed at any cost, a cold hearted killer that kept those under him perpetually in fear through dark deeds and violence, nothing too sadistic for his tastes, a brief glimpse of reality suddenly shone through Prtzillines' mind on noticing all those around him try to subtly distance themselves. There and then, he knew it was over and that his fifty year rule had come to an end, not at all how he'd imagined it. Frustrated, angry, full of what he perceived as righteous vengeance at being dethroned by this smug and conceited intruder that assumed he knew what was best for not only his land, but the world at large, being held in captivity like a chained up animal was never really going to be an option for him. And so, in one final act in which he thought he could reap some kind of revenge on not only these new assailants, but his turncoat subjects that were even now separating themselves from him, he scoured his mind for the darkest magic he knew and prepared to go out all guns blazing.

Pleased with himself at having ignored his friend's specific request not to bring any part of his army, as usual, foreseeing events before they'd even happened, planning for any and every contingency, a small but insistent niggling at the back of For'son's mind suddenly called for his attention. Not one to ignore a prompt from his consciousness, no matter how trivial, the warrior dragon flooded himself with all his supernatural power and stretched out with his senses, attuning himself to everything in the immediate vicinity.

Abruptly a myriad of brilliant, colourful, bright life swam across his mind in every different direction. Dragonflies nestling atop long strands of grass resembled statues as they tried to remain out of sight. Fireflies zipped in and out of the reeds, their exquisite twilight colours negated by the daylight, none bothered at all by the presence of a prehistoric army suddenly turning up on their doorstep. Beneath the surface of the murky water, snapping turtles, normally not afraid of anything, due in part to their armoured shells, scattered in every direction, the commotion all too much for even them. Fish in all shapes and sizes gracefully glided off towards more peaceful parts of the quagmire, seeking solitude and safe haven. Nesting birds watched eerily on, afraid of the huge beings that they'd never even realised existed before the unfolding events of today, afraid for their lives, though determined not to abandon their precious eggs. And then there were the dragons, over five and a half thousand, their presences all standing out in his mind, each one different to the next in innumerable ways. Those on their side projected an overwhelming sense of steeliness, in the main focused, a reassuring sense of honour and their willingness to die for their monarch cutting through the darkness like a lighthouse in the most tropical of storms. In stark contrast, the auras of those on the other side were barely visible, their wills almost crushed, having been subjugated for far too long. One or two sparkled occasionally though, tiny dots of hope scrambling for something to cling on to, thoughts of reuniting with their families and a brighter future no doubt rattling through their minds. And then he caught the briefest of glimpses of it, standing on its own, the others now giving it a wide berth.

'Prtzillines,' he thought, sensing a build up within the leader that they'd tried in vain to turn to their way of thinking. Forward, progressive and sane were things he most certainly wasn't, leading them straight down this path to the point of no return. Ignoring everything else within his sphere of influence, the king's friend focused all his ethereal attention on the lethal leader. Bold, and particularly obvious now that he knew what to look for, the more For'son studied what was before him, the more he got a sense of something magical going on inside the adversarial dragon. Pretty sure he knew what it was, instantly he snapped his attention back to the harsh reality around them, wondering what he could do to counteract the inevitable.

Grim thoughts gripping his mind, unable to believe that it had come to this, the concept of surrender was something he was ill equipped to deal with, having always used violence, even from an early age, to take what he wanted. Scared now that his wicked endeavours had finally caught up with him, all he could think to do was lash out and be damned, the consequences of such action not even occurring to him. He had after all, never thought too far ahead.

And so in the middle of the boggy swamp, under the radiant warm rays of the blazing hot sun, anger roaring inside him like a two hundred foot raging waterfall leaping off a mountain, Prtzillines inundated himself with magic and in one final act of contempt and rage, gave in to his vicious temper.

Fierce and loyal, the king's dragons were ready for anything, or at least they thought they were. And despite their single-mindedness, their superior numbers and motivation to protect the monarch, they were still all very much caught unaware.

Appearing out of nowhere, encompassing the ferocious leader's cruel and nasty form, dazzling blue tendrils of electrical energy forked and crackled through the air, setting it, the ground all around, and those in the immediate vicinity on fire. As magic went it was spectacular, lavish, extravagant, unrestrained and wasteful. No dragon, however mighty, could fuel such power for very long, something Prtzillines knew and couldn't have cared less about. With his former subjects scattering like chickens sensing the fox arriving at the hen house, some trying to take flight, others sprinting through the muddy water for all they were worth, the deranged dragon, feeling as though he had no other alternative, loaded himself up with ethereal energy, and in a streaking, deadly blue blur, tore across the ground towards the king, scattering and shocking the fearsome protectors in the process.

Alert and on guard, ready for what he thought was anything, nothing could have prepared For'son for what appeared out of nowhere in front of him.

'How in the...?' was all he had time to think before all hell broke loose.

Reacting as only he could, all the time admiring whatever supernatural hex or spell the dark dragon leader had conjured up in his boiling rage, the king's friend and of course guardian reinforced every single one of his scales from the well of ethereal energy that filled his soul, and enhancing his speed with just a smidgen of power, set course to see if he could intercept the danger before it got anywhere near his sovereign.

Wafting across the mire, the overpowering smell of roasted flesh (or in this case, scales) from the thousands of miniscule lightning strikes against the overwhelming dragon force had every single creature fleeing for their lives. A splashing watery chaos, the likes of which the ground there had never seen, was only really the start of things, because as you probably realise, electricity and water do not mix under any circumstances, even as far back in history as this.

Lurching forward, the desire to protect their king engrained within them, those prehistoric monsters between him and the leader of this land leapt into action, some sprinting into the fray, others bounding into the air, skimming the surface of their watery surroundings, each with the aim of taking out the threat once and for all. But all of them were to some degree or other... WET!

Knowing that once it got going, he'd decimate hundreds of dragons, having once destroyed a whole village who'd gone against him and had continued using the hot springs located near their settlement at the edge of his land in much the same way, so as to set an example, he had little understanding of why the magic interacted with the water in that way, only that it did and because of that he would make many of them pay. Heading straight for the king of the newcomers at speed, shocking most of those that approached him into submission with the blindingly bright, arcing lightning that hummed through the air in every direction all around him, the rapture of so much magic coursing through his veins was almost too much to take... ALMOST!

About to get stuck in, his fiery magic lit up like the surface of the sun, it was only when he witnessed the first of the dragons freezing stock still, unable to move, in agonising pain, that he realised something was dreadfully wrong. And that led him to take an extra moment, one which could potentially lead to the king's downfall, to assess the situation more fully. Barely able to comprehend the unusual magic he was seeing for the first time, something that in itself shocked him to his very core because he considered himself a master of all things supernatural, it was only when another nagging feeling at the back of his mind pointed him in the right direction that For'son started to get a handle on exactly what was going on.

"'The water,' he thought, taking in the effect the dragon-made lightning was having on those all around. 'The water is what's causing the carnage.'

Dropping like flies (dragon flies... get it?), dozens of dragons surrounding the monarch had succumbed to the blistering electrical effects of the unrecognisable magic, some frozen solid, others slumped on the floor, their hearts stopped, their bodies still sizzling away, as Prtzillines closed in.

Now the king was one of the mightiest warriors the world had ever known, but even he was backing away slowly, eyes wide open in surprise at what was coming for him, sloshing the water in and around his legs as he did so.

'What would it do without the water?' was just one of the many questions ringing out in For'son's head as he watched impending doom approach, but it was probably the most important one. Knowing that he had to act quickly, the gravity of what he would do not lost on him at all, especially not with his friend's life on the line, the brave and fearsome warrior gambled on a strategy that appeared utterly bizarre. Mind set on a course of action, without hesitation he whirled into action, knowing full well that what he'd decided on might not work. It was a guess, that's all, but an educated one. And so, whispering the words of a mantra he'd chosen in his mind, and more importantly putting all his considerable willpower behind them, he allowed his magic to work its... MAGIC, and waited to see if his gamble paid off.

Both frightening and majestic, dragons had ruled the earth for as long as time could remember, and despite getting on a bit, occasionally walking into a room and forgetting the reason why, Time did for the most part have excellent recall.

Roaming the globe in all different shapes, sizes and colours, the prehistoric scaled goliaths remain the planet's apex predator no matter what the continent. Take China for example. The dragons there are more serpent-like creatures, with long elongated bodies, multi-hued limbs and have a capacity to control the rain with ancient magic passed down through the generations, most with either small wings or none at all, preferring instead to stay firmly attached to the ground. Still, they are top of the food chain. Across Korea, long bearded dragons fly freely, claims of omnipotence abound derived from their particular brand of supernatural, devouring everything in their way, nothing big enough to pose even a minute threat.

Throughout the waters surrounding both Northern and Southern poles, grandiose water dragons surf the white crested waves, delve deep underwater, hunkering down below the ice.

Across Europe and Scandinavia more conventional dragons wander the land, including the geothermal underground, meandering through the sky, feasting on flocks of sheep and cattle at will, generally ignoring the savage bipeds that know little of how to cover themselves up, or even the rudimentary skill of making fire.

All of them have one thing in common... MAGIC! Born with it, an ethereal spark passed on from generation to generation, those few atoms that reside inside their eggs before they are hatched are enough to cascade into powerful brilliance much later on in life, and combined with just enough education about how to harness it effectively and how best to channel it efficiently, have led to a race of beings that, between them, nearly rule the world. Over time, mantras, or spells and hexes if you prefer to use the other terms, have come into being, passed down, recorded, there for all to learn, enhancing abilities, squeezing out every last drop of magic, making it as potent as possible. There are a few other races that come close to matching the outright might and supernatural power of the dragons... the basilisks, the nagas, the manticores, the heretics of Antar, the hydra, and the unicorn lookalikes the ra-hoon, but the magic of all these beings is not nearly as ancient or potent. And so for the most part, dragons rule. If there's a part of the world they aren't in charge of, it's because they don't want it, very much like the Poles previously mentioned. There the environments are so cold, no dragon could survive even with their powerful abilities, and so they don't rule there, not yet anyway, leaving the way free for the hydra and the nagas to duke it out. Every other temperate part of the planet is theirs though apart from a couple. If events today could be turned around, and this land brought under the flag of the king and his domain, there would be only one outstanding realm left resisting the rule of democracy and the will of the dragons... Ahrensburg!

It happened in a split second, and felt like the exact opposite of... RAIN! The water on the ground, amongst the grass, soaking beings in a radius of fifty wingspans all of a sudden took off into the air in the form of tiny droplets. An upside down deluge if you like. As the moments ticked by, every last molecule of moisture leapt skyward, drying out everything, the world's first magical tumble dryer. As a hot arid heat clenched its fist around For'son, Prtzillines, the king and the rest of his army, mouths ran dry, scales became less supple, all against the

27

backdrop of the thunderous roar of the dazzling forked lightning that had by now become much less forceful and effective. Yes, it burnt deep into the surrounding dragon's bodies, scorching scales, inflicting excruciating pain, throwing some of them off their feet, ripping and tearing wings, drilling holes through sinew and muscle. But in the dry, arid, moisture free environment, what it didn't do was electrocute. And that was enough for a brave dragon like For'son to act. So he did, with all of his ability.

Conjuring up an almighty gust of wind, he threw it against the lightning shrouded monster that still headed towards the king. Caught off guard, the dreaded leader of this land, inflictor of pain and suffering since long ago had his feet taken out from under him, his wings of little use due to the unsuspecting nature of the attack. Dumped unceremoniously to the bone dry floor, in two bounds the king's protector and friend was upon the hell bent Prtzillines, pummelling his head with a flurry of magically imbued punches, bright green viscous blood teeming from his battered knuckles, all the time roaring a blistering cone of flame into the monster's face, while absorbing the bone crunching lightning strikes that gnawed and nibbled at every part of his body. Moments later it was over, the sadistic dark dragon put out of his misery for good, his skull fully charred, burnt to a cinder, the flickering bolts of harsh electricity being absorbed by the smoky sweltering air. Only then did it occur to the hero of the hour, the defeater of the dark, that other beings there were suffering.

With all the moisture gone, and the ground all around them having run dry, fish and other aquatic life gulped and gasped, desperate for the very life force that allowed them to exist. Two words... that's all it took to bring forth a deluge of epic proportions, flooding just the area that had been affected, that and no more. Cooling burnt and scorched scales, the supernatural rain was something of a relief to all those affected by the suicidal attack from the former leader of this land.

Momentarily stunned at the close shave he'd just avoided, opening up his mind, the dragon king reached out using his innate telepathic ability and ordered those healers within his army to get straight to work, reminding them to not only care for their own, but those from what had been the other side, making sure they got the treatment they needed.

Strolling casually over to his friend, who was now, much like some of the other dragons, rolling himself in the thick clear water that he'd brought down from the sky, the monarch of the world and now conqueror of this land pulled up short, smiling at the sight in front of him.

"Your default position always seems to be needing a bath. Why is that?"

"Perhaps sire, because I do all your dirty work for you," replied For'son playfully.

"Smart arse!"

"I cannot deny it, Majesty," replied the king's friend, rising to his feet, shaking off the water much in the same way a shaggy dog would do after a dip in the sea.

"That was an extraordinary show of power," observed the king. "Thoughts?"

"Hmmm..." considered For'son carefully. "If I had to guess, I'd say it mimicked lightning right down to its very base structure. How he achieved such a thing though, is quite beyond me."

Nodding ever so slightly, the head of state looked perplexed and sad in equal measure.

"But now that we know what can be conjured into existence, there's no reason not to try and replicate it. And perhaps some of our newly gained allies can give us a head start in that direction."

"Good thinking," added the king. "If we can somehow reproduce exactly the power that he had, we could document it, and hopefully create a series of mantras for future generations. That would be something worthwhile working towards."

"Agreed sire," replied For'son, much more formal now that other dragons were milling about. "I'll take a portion of the army and escort our new friends back to their capital and set about repairing the damage done by that psychopath," he said, indicating the now deceased dragon leader, floating face up in the watery ground.

"Good," replied the king. "I've already ordered the diplomats and politicians to head that way in an effort to smooth things over, appoint a new leader and start the clean up. All things being equal, they should arrive at about the same time. And as if you need telling, don't forget to check out their library, should they have one. That might give us a clue about how he brought forth the lightning and offer up an insight into any other surprising magic that they have access to. Once again, you've done great work, if not a little unconventional at times. I will remind you as I always do on these occasions... I don't like being kept in the dark!"

"You say that," whispered For'son conspiratorially, "but you know you love it really and can't wait to see what the surprise will be. Admit it... it all adds to the thrill."

'Damn!' thought the king, 'he knows me too well.'

"You might be right," the monarch whispered back, "but just occasionally it would be nice to be assured victory in advance and not go through all that squeaky bum time. And next time," he commanded, "make sure you're the bait!"

Standing in the middle of the swamp, nearly up to his knees in water, the wildlife having all disappeared off in every direction, the king's friend started off with a chuckle, which almost immediately turned into a giggle, soon becoming a guffaw, after which uncontrollable hysterics took over, attracting the attention of every dragon there, much to their bemusement.

"You're quite insane. Sometimes I'm still not sure why I keep you around," the king leaned in and said. "What is it that's so funny?"

"A... squeaky royal bum," sniggered For'son, "that's a picture I won't be able to erase from my mind in a hurry."

Shaking his head in bewilderment, fully appreciating all aspects of his friend's diverse and bizarre personality, the sovereign turned and strolled towards the commander of his army, who was attempting to bring his adversaries over to their way of thinking with, by the looks of things, a great deal of success. After only a few paces, the monarch turned fully back around, and with a smile on his face, shouted,

"Don't forget... NO MORE USING ME AS BAIT! UNDERSTOOD?"

Still tittering in amusement, tears of laughter splashing down his prehistoric scaled face, the king's friend nodded and replied,

"Understood!"

And that was pretty much that. Over the course of the next twenty four hours, a significant number of dragons converged on Prtzillines' former land, providing food, care, guidance, instilling the inhabitants there with belief that a new, kinder way of life was theirs for the taking, and that under the king's watchful eye, dragons across the planet would not only survive, but flourish. Given what they'd all been through, how they'd been subjugated, tortured and abused physically and mentally, it didn't take much to win them over, really only a kind touch. So it was, with only a handful of deaths, that the dragon domain king, Greger being his given name, had struck a real victory, turning darkness into light, freeing unjustly treated dragons in all but a day, something of a miracle given the circumstances. All of this took place across an area that today would be regarded as the northern two thirds of Italy, just to give you a geographical idea of where we're dealing with. Back then though, the architecture of the world looked very different, with some of the great seas landlocked, and whole continents merging together. For the dragons, the mighty rulers of most of the planet, it didn't really matter as quite a lot of their time was spent underground, colonising vast subterranean caverns, turning them into rudimentary cities, linking them up with gigantic flying tunnels, using their magic and vast knowledge to warm everything up to their liking, with the plentiful supply of roiling hot lava and geothermal energy playing a huge part in exactly that.

Over the course of a week, For'son, acting as the king's deputy, alongside the diplomats and politicians transformed the land's capital and outlying regions, making sure that no dragon went hungry, magically fixing dwellings that had become run down, eventually capping all this off with appointing a new leader of the land, one of their own, elected in a fair and democratic way, a dragon that would not only govern that area, but would attend worldwide council meetings regularly, giving the denizens there a voice, something they very much liked the idea of. The only real struggle was the concept of introducing the rule of law, something most of them had never known, well... not in its proper form, only tyranny from the sadistic monster that could change his mind on a whim, murdering in moments, torturing for no apparent reason, doing whatever the hell he wanted to in order to satisfy his sick appetites. Abiding by an agreed set of regulations that conformed across the world was just so foreign and alien to these dragons, that disagreements, clashes and conflict became inevitable, even with the newly elected leader coming down strongly on the side of reform. In the end, the newly freed citizens came round to the idea, but it wasn't easy, with it being evident there would be many bumps in the road along the way. In what little free time he had, which wasn't much, a measly few hours in the early hours of the morning, For'son dropped everything and followed one of his chief passions, as the king suggested, and known all along that without a doubt, he'd be headed down that road, off to what the locals regarded as their repository of supernatural information, or to you and me, the library.

It was a laugh that it could be regarded as such, because in physical terms, it was only really an offshoot of one of the caves that they stored all of their food in for winter, and a grubby and horrid one at that. Full to the brim with spiders, rats and numerous different insect species, it broke the king's friend's heart that any kind of knowledge was stored in a place like this, as the warrior had a great respect for anything written down, knowing that it was essential to the future. Libraries and their contents would no doubt play a huge part in the development of his race in the coming centuries, of that he was absolutely certain. Their understanding and thirst for information about absolutely everything would be what kept them at the top of the food chain and maintain their position as rulers of the planet.

Brushing away monstrous spider webs in front of him, ducking down as low as he could go in an effort to get his huge dragon frame into what to him appeared to be nothing more than a closet, he strolled into what supposedly passed for the repository here. Immediately his heart dropped. Why? Because of the state of things... tattered scrolls with illegible scribble littered the floor, some with parts torn off, others stained from the damp, clearly of no use to anyone. Lighting the candles around the room with the most delicate squirts of flame he could manage from between his mighty jaws, the ferocious fighter, now very much in scholar mode, perused the furthest corners and the pathetic looking piles of tomes stacked up almost to chest height. As with the scrolls, they were nearly all damaged or broken in some way, shape or form, with covers missing, pages ripped or the ink inside stained or smudged so badly that nothing could be made of the contents within. Anger and sadness vied for dominance within him as he tried to understand how anyone, least of all sentient beings of his own kind, could treat their history and their intelligence like this. Barbaric was really all he could come up with to explain what lay all around in front of him. Clearly there was much here, some of which could shed extraordinary light on the land itself, the local customs and even, he was sure, some of their unusual magic. But to make head or tail of it all seemed an almost impossible task given the dire state of the documents. But after, well... not so much sulking, but feeling sorry for himself and the collection of written words, he pushed on, and like the conscientious dragon that he was, sat down and started to sort his way through every last scrap of parchment and paper. It took the best part of a week working through the night, every night, after which he'd consigned everything of even vague importance, magic or otherwise, to his eidetic memory and had thoroughly tidied and catalogued the entire room, repairing what he could, discarding the waste, some of which he was sure would have been valuable had it not been damaged beyond belief. Only then did he gather those in charge in an effort to explain the importance of the magic repository, using all his skills in an effort to make them understand. They said that they did, and that they would protect the material within the tiny cave, but only a small part of him believed them. He hoped they would, and that they could, over time, garner enough experience and knowledge to add to the collection, making it warrant a much bigger and safer new home. Knowing that he'd done all he could, his thoughts focused on finishing his tasks there, eager now to get home and rejoin his friend, the monarch.

And so with the vast majority of politicians, diplomats and troops staying behind to help with setting up the local government, the judiciary, policing, contacting the outer reaches of the land and other more mundane tasks, the king's friend and protector set off home, knowing that at least for now, things were under control and that the new land, all its residents, as well as the world itself were benefiting significantly from the change in leadership.

Choosing to fly above ground all the way, preferring

the sun on his wings and scales rather than being cooped up in the newly built, sometimes claustrophobic underground tunnels, keen to get back to some sense of normality, it took him five hours to return, flying at a leisurely pace. He stopped a couple of times, once to devour a whole sheep, tiny strands of wool from its coat even now stuck in between a few of his back molars, just niggling away at him, on the other occasion taking down a fully grown deer, something that proved much more of a challenge, especially given the sheer scale of its antlers and just how sharp they'd been. Despite his hugely advantageous size, he'd had to fight tooth and nail to take down the buck, incurring heavy scratching around his antediluvian jaw and nose, risking partial blindness if he got it wrong. But that was part of the thrill, earning the right to eat and making the meal taste that much more sumptuous. Of course, he could have used his divine supernatural abilities to snag it in a heartbeat, but that's not how it's done, at least not in his mind. Hunting for food should be exactly that... HUNTING! It shouldn't be done with just a thought and the flick of a finger or a couple of words reinforced with a dash of will. NO! Exercising primal instincts, the thrill of the hunt, following what was thoroughly embedded in a dragon's DNA, that's what it's all about, as well as respecting the prey that you take down, even those that don't fight back, like that sheep. He knew that some dragons did it... use magic to hunt. As far as he was concerned though, it made them weak, stupid and lazy, something he most certainly wasn't.

Landing as light as a feather on a solid rock plateau on the periphery of the capital, just inside the fortifications, on what would now be regarded as central London, his glistening bright blue crystalline scales shivered ever so slightly on hitting a wave of blustery cold air that currently encompassed the seat of power in the true dragon capital. Choosing to walk instead of fly, his extensive wings aching from the journey home, especially across the water due in main to the rough weather, For'son, assuming an air of authority, headed for the main underground entrance to the governmental part of the brightly lit conurbation, passing ordinary dragons going about their normal lives in every shape, scale and colour, acknowledging them with a nod as he did so.

'What a wonderful world we live in,' he mused, strolling down a polished rock sidewalk, not even needing to squeeze past others going in the opposite direction, so big was the space allowed. Briefly he wondered when it had become this way. Certainly not as far back as his youth, that's for sure. Then it was all about roaming the countryside, sticking to your side of the fence, metaphorically speaking, because of course no known fence could contain even the most feeble of dragons. 'About the last hundred years or so,' he assumed, answering his own question. First the villages and remote outposts in this great land had come together in a way not ever known before, after that, well... cooperation on a phenomenal scale, across their land anyway. Teaming up had brought good fortune in all sorts of ways. From the sharing of different and ancient magic, to knowledge about construction, healing, food and diet, thoughts on how best to take care of the young, pushing the boundaries of what could be done aerially, as well as a history shared, revealing much about those that had gone before them and best of all, a willingness to learn from both their mistakes and triumphs. Remarkable in such a short space of time, only enhanced and developed further by the vision to incorporate not just the dragons of other countries, but the entire planet, providing peace and sustainability for every single being. A lofty goal for sure, but now they were on the verge of completing their epic adventure, with just Ahrensburg to go. Just... that was a laugh he knew, nodding at the half dozen guards defending the inner gate to what they all thought of as the citadel of power, the place where once every other month councillors, or their representatives at least, met to discuss the world's politics, promoting bright new ideas, brainstorming how to go forward and what else they could possibly do to enlighten this brave new world. Thinking about all this forced his chest out as far as it would go, like a proud peacock strutting his stuff, his fabulous blue hues not dissimilar to the bird itself. Cutting his way through throngs of his own race, the underground inside not affording nearly the same amount of space as up above, like a dragon on a mission he headed directly for his friend's office, hoping to grab a quick word.

The wickedly hot heat nibbling at his feet forced him to look down to the floor, marvelling at what he saw. Just visible through the tiny crisscrossing cracks in the stone, intense orange, red and yellow colours swirled and twirled, twisted and writhed, the visceral molten magma a magnet for his mind, drawn towards it, lost in its stunning beauty, elegance and most of all, the radiant heat that it gave off. It was difficult to continue in a straight line. What was odd, he thought, was having the lava there, giving off the sumptuous heat and light, without the effect of the noxious fumes that normally accompanied it. It was a recent development of a timeworn concept, and something the engineers of the capital were exceptionally proud of, he knew. With so many new skills and ideas adding to the pre-existing multitude of magic and innovation on almost a daily basis, from the fresh lands being integrated into the king's vision of an all encompassing brave new world, the possibilities were almost endless. And that had led to the dragon council forming a committee to oversee original developments that would enhance the basic dragon way of life. Small things, granted, but ones that would provide hope, comfort, relief and separate dragonkind from mindless beasts that roam the countryside. Heating some of the much larger parts of the capital using the molten magma that much of it is built upon was just one of those ideas. Easy in theory, that is until you have to account for the toxic fumes that still present a threat, even to the ever resilient dragons. And so it was that only a couple of years ago, the brightest minds from across all the incorporated lands had come up with a magical filter that allows the heat and light to pass straight up through the cracks in the paving, whilst at the same time captures the billowing poisonous vapours, before nullifying them completely. Complicated magic executed perfectly, that's how the monarch had described this one undertaking, spreading details of it to outposts across the globe, allowing all and sundry to reap the rewards of this new found partnership. And that was just the start, already there was more in the offing. New and innovative ways to carve through rock were already being developed alongside food production on a vast scale, including a plan to create one of the staples of dragon life, charcoal, on an industrial scale. Rumours also abounded about a system to provide drinking water to each abode in every city, as well as a cross planet, interconnecting series of flying tunnels that would allow dragons to travel anywhere at any time, negating the elemental elements on the surface such as storms, cyclones and other kinds of weather related events that would hinder travel by air. Progress was thick and fast, something that at times made For'son's head spin just thinking about it, but as far as he was concerned, it was all very much an improvement on what they had before, when different tribes constantly waged war against each other, savagery of the worst kind, dragon versus dragon, maiming, killing indiscriminately when there was no real need to do so, only because they'd known no other way. And he was old enough to remember... JUST! Enlightenment hadn't come quickly or easily, but now here it was very much welcomed. If only they could sort out the one land remaining, then their goal could be realised and a suitable era of peace could really begin. But the regular reports of what was happening inside Ahrensburg, smuggled out through an audacious and completely secret pipeline of complicit beings made for fear inspiring reading. Wicked deeds compounded by a sickening brutality were commonplace across the land's major communities on an hourly basis. Of course their leader was the worst culprit, with those under him coming in a close second, ruling by fear, culling those unbelievers showing even the remotest doubt, torture, mental invasion, sadistic games and MURDER all routine.

Shaking his head, continuing on his way through the twisty maze of corridors, all the time wondering how on earth they were going to solve the conundrum that was the last land to be wrestled out from viciousness, cruelty and ignorance, the fierce protector strode into an open auditorium full of his bustling prehistoric kind, work continuing at a pace.

'Ahh... the monument,' he mused, wondering how much it had come along since he'd last been here. 'A great deal,' he thought, judging from the ever increasing height and width of it all, hidden behind the dark brown makeshift barricades that had been introduced by the artisan crafters in charge of the project.

The king, known for his appreciation and support of the arts in whatever their form, from dragon opera (something that just has to be heard... think a roaring pride of lions gargling glass with indiscriminate snarls of flame thrown into the mix, times ten, and then you might be somewhere close to the right ballpark), cave paintings and tapestry, to some of the finer philosophical tomes ever penned. Keen to keep up to date and appear a modern free thinker, he'd been convinced to sign off on the commission of a huge statue that would represent all that he'd achieved in bringing so much of the planet together. The idea was that it would be finished and presented once the final piece of the puzzle was put into place... Ahrensburg!

Wondering just how they were going to go about bringing that last land into the fold, For'son's mind wandered back to the artisans and what they were doing. Part of him yearned to let go of his constricted thoughts and just be free, free to do whatever he liked, to express himself in... he didn't know. Paint sounded fun, or clay, yes... he liked the sound of that. Singing though, most certainly did not. He and most definitely his voice were not designed to be listened to by others, especially not for their pleasure, besides which the thought of standing in front of dragons, trying to manipulate his vocal chords sent a shiver of cold sweat coursing from top to bottom of his scaled tail.

Shaping metal... that appealed more than a little. Growing up, he'd spent many an hour in the forge, soaking up the heat, roiling in sweat, mesmerised by the hot coals changing colour. The darkest black possible slowly gobbled up by the yellow, and then orange and at the height, a sunrise red, set off behind the wavering hot air, allowing the smiths to work their magic, shape the metal, bend and twist that which would otherwise be unmoveable, before time turned what was left to a pale, ashen dust. Intoxicating, that's what he thought on reliving the memory. What it would be to toil at the forge every day, allow your imagination to run wild, to create... what? Humungous deadly weapons for dragons to wield sounded a little too much. Of course a tiny part of him liked to be armed when it all kicked off, generally something oversized, like a gigantic double-sided axe, a halberd, a scythe or a sickle, all of which over the years he'd used to great effect when necessary. But that's not the direction in which his mind guided him, right here, right now, as he strolled on towards his friend's office. Creating fantastical shapes, shimmering and unusual surfaces, structures that had no real meaning or use, all from the visions of his mind's eye, called to his very nature, which was odd because there were few dragons braver or, when it called for it, more vicious. That side of him only raised its head on the occasions when his friends were in dire trouble or when lives needed to be saved, whether from a brutal dictator or some overwhelming emergency. Up until now, the creative side of his personality had never once shown its face, and given the work he had to do to bring Ahrensburg on side in one last effort to bring peace to the planet, it was unlikely at best that it was going to stick around for very long. And then it struck him, in very much the same way that the hammer in that forge walloped the metal, pounding it into shape, inch by inch, crushing the straight, pummelling the metal's natural tendencies, altering and improving every dynamic fundamentally, until finally beauty and functionality combined to produce the magnificent. Caught up in that special place deep within his mind where a dragon's magic resides, he could see himself at the forge, hear the pulverising of the ore, feel the heat battering his body, sweat pouring off every scale as his muscles ached beyond belief. But instead of producing massive mighty weapons that would complement him in battle, he could just make out statues and structures all with the same theme, one that he loved more than all others, one that gave him the solace that he needed at times, healing his very soul, filling him with purpose, making him believe anything was possible... THE SEA!

Rolling waves made out of metal surrounding the polished stone on the floor all about the forge. Some that could fit in the palm of your hand, others taller than the bipeds that flourished across the world, putting their uneducated stamp on it if you like. Silver, bronze, brass and, even one (the smallest, due to how rare and valuable it was) made of laminium, a substance that has the ability to enhance a dragon's magic, one found in microscopic amounts across the world, generally in much colder climates, making it that much more difficult to get hold of because of the mind-numbing effect chilly weather has on their prehistoric bodies. Willing his vision to close in on the tiny metallic sculpture, for once it obeyed, moving up close, enabling him to see the most minute of details. The crest of the wave looked like perfection, so lost was he in the writhing curves, caught up in the realistic movement, the glint of water turning into powerful white foam, almost making it possible for him to smell the salty fresh air that he so longed for.

Abruptly, he was snapped away from his crafting thoughts and back to reality as a familiar voice welcomed him home.

"My friend," declared the king on seeing him walk through the door, "it's so good to see you. How was your journey back?"

"Good sire, thank you for asking."

"And I suppose you snuck off to some beach or other before coming straight here."

More of a statement than a question, it was only really then that he realised just how well his friend knew him, probably better than he knew himself in fact.

"Well... I might have stopped to... you know, take a comfort break. When you reach my time of life, things downstairs start to get a little wobbly and unreliable. Oh what I'd give to have the body of a dragon half my age."

"Hmmm..." uttered the monarch, not believing a word of it.

"And just how are my new subjects faring?"

"They're doing pretty well, all things considered. I think it will take them some time to grasp the rule of law, and its consequences, but apart from that, they're making great strides in the right direction. Over the course of the week or so that I was there, it was easy to see the change not only in dynamic but in attitude. From being downtrodden and fearful of everything, by the time I left genuine laughter and smiles were abundantly clear from nearly every being there. It was heart warming to see such a drastic change in the right direction, Majesty."

"Good work my friend, and that extends to the others there. I'll make my feelings known to them when they come back. Did you find out anything useful in your travels?"

"You mean did they have a library, and did I scour it mercilessly every night that I was there?"

"Something like that," chuckled the sovereign, unable to put it better himself.

"They did, and I did," replied his friend, all the time smiling.

"And..."

"After sorting through a whole host of dross, I'm pretty sure I've uncovered some unpolished gems."

"Is that so?"

"Sure is. Watch this," announced the mighty, blue shaded dragon.

Taking a breath, whilst at the same time composing himself, he stretched out one of his spindly looking fingers, and using the words from one of the scrolls that he'd found, one that he'd already tried to make sure that it worked, with just a tiny dribble of magic, trying not to be reckless at all... let rip. Suddenly, a purple tinged fork of bright green lightning arced across the room, splitting a tiny clay replica of the king on a shelf over twenty five metres away, sending shards scattering in every direction, the accompanying BOOM and CRASH bringing dragons running from all directions, much to the monarch's dismay.

"Excellent," replied Greger, the dragon king, more than a little sarcastically, before dismissing all those onlookers that had just arrived.

"And before you say it, I'm just off to see Orac in the library so that I can add it all to his growing collection," smiled his friend, pleased at his little demonstration, having never really liked that particular piece of art.

Shaking his head at his pal's showing off, all the monarch could say was,

"He will be pleased."

"How will we know?" answered For'son mischievously,

over his shoulder, well aware of the fact that the stoic librarian rarely smiled.

"Cut him some slack," ordered the king, slightly more seriously than intended. "He's been through a great deal, alright. And without him, things down there would be a mess."

"I know, I know," reflected For'son. "I was only joking. He's a good being to have around in times of peace or crisis, and I'd trust him to have my back, that alone should tell you how highly I regard him."

"It does," answered the king, pleased to see his friend slightly more serious.

"Anyhow," announced the crystalline blue, freshly returned mighty warrior, "I'm off downstairs to the library. If you need me, that's where I'll be. Catch you later."

And with that, he gave a respectful nod, before turning on the spot and heading off towards the nearest open chute that would allow him to gracefully glide down two levels to where the library was located.

Fighting against the roaring wind and the stinging rain, across what would now be regarded as the North Sea, but was at this time much, much more than that, a bold, daring and courageous female dragon was having one hell of a time of it. Exquisitely coloured golden wings gave all that they had to propel the beautiful female on, muscles and tendons burning like the touch of the hottest lava, provoking the fiercest pain she'd ever known to inundate her mind, causing her momentarily to squeal out in agony, not that it could be heard over the harsh howls of the monstrous wind that she found herself caught up in. Sticking out like a sore thumb, her golden, yellow and orange brilliance against the darkest black and grey clouds and the nightmarish shadowy water below topped off by devilishly white foam, fought for all she was worth as the thunderous growl of the vicious waves crashing together continued in one long symphony. Had anyone but the elements been there to witness her epic battle, it would have been obvious to them that the gorgeous prehistoric beast was losing her fight, which compounded matters a great deal you see, because she was carrying an urgent message for the monarch of this world, an important one about an unruly species from her home land that had started taking dragons against their will, and turning them to their side without the slightest hesitation. How it had been done was a mystery to the best minds amongst her kind in the homeland that she loved above all else. If they were to succeed in vanquishing these dastardly foes, then the only solution lay with the king and the bright minds in the capital, somewhere she was headed for at her fastest speed possible. And then, from out of nowhere, this storm had appeared and seemingly dashed all her chances. But even though the circumstances were dire, she soldiered on, pushing away the pain, battling the driving wind and the squally gusts, ignoring the rain pelting her magnificent scales, using her massive tail as a giant rudder to steer her in the right direction. Concentrating only on the next flap of her wings, she doubled her resolve, thoughts only of those of her land, and howling like a banshee whose privates had been caught in a bear trap, pushed ever forward.

"Orac," ventured For'son, on entering the multi-roomed library that seemed to have gained at least another three or four dozen aisles of books in his absence.

"For'son," grumbled the distinctly shy and retiring librarian who'd been tasked with putting the library together and making it the most astounding and complete magical repository of its kind on the planet.

Without looking up from the text that he was reading, just sensing the dragon he regarded as reckless and impulsive standing there waiting to be seen to, he knew there was no getting out of it.

"What can I do for you?" he asked, not really wanting to and more than a bit miffed at being interrupted, not for the first time today.

"I've just arrived back. Did you hear about the battle?"

"I did," replied the librarian, head still buried in a book.

"What do you think... is it worth noting down for future generations?"

"Is that the only reason that you're here?" asked Orac, slamming the dusty red tome with ancient silver hieroglyphics embedded into the cover, firmly shut, an insignificant act that showed just how much he was irked.

"Come on... you know it makes sense, on so many levels. If you're keen to detail it, I'll gladly sit with you and recount it from my point of view."

"I bet you would."

"What's that supposed to mean?"

"It means... that all you're looking for is the glory that comes along with such deeds. For once, why don't you come to me with a selfless act, one truly worthy of taking down and preserving for future generations?"

"Are you saying that I'm not worthy?" added For'son, starting to get put out.

If the timid librarian noticed, it didn't show.

"Not you yourself, but your actions. You're, by your own admission, a fighter, a dragon taken to following your baser instincts, letting your bloodlust control your temper, attitude and in particular, your actions. I'm not here to catalogue all of that, because if I was, there'd be too much for me to take note of."

"If not that, then what?"

"I think you already know, For'son. Use that deeply developed brain to either outwit your opponent or settle things peacefully."

"But... but... but..."

"Yes... I know that you did, to some degree. But you still murdered their leader, is that not right?"

Swallowing nervously, something of a new experience to our brave royal protector, For'son pondered his reply.

"That was more out of necessity than anything else. If there'd been another way, then I'd obviously have taken it."

"It's always the same story with you. Don't get me wrong," continued Orac, "I greatly admire what you do, and your dedication to not only your job, but the monarch as well. I just wish sometimes you would use your brain to outthink your opponent and come to a peaceful resolution. After all, that is the whole point of what we're doing, trying to bring peace to the entire world as we know it, for the benefit of every living creature."

"Not sheep though, or cows," uttered For'son, only half sarcastically, referring to two of his favourite snacks.

The librarian offered up a withering glare in return for his remark.

"You know what I mean."

"I do, and I'm sorry. But with Ahrensburg remaining very much untamed, I think a non violent solution to THAT problem is as out of reach as the moon or the sun."

"But you don't know that," ventured Orac. "How do you know before you even try?"

'Under normal circumstances,' thought For'son, 'he'd be right.' But they as a united front had history with Ahrensburg, a very bloody and brutal one at that. Diplomatically, everything had been tried, over and over again, all to no avail. Scouts and even ambassadors that had been sent by the king himself had been sadistically slain for just daring to approach their borders, their viciously tortured bodies strung up for all to see outside of their lands, a warning to others about approaching, something taken heed of by the king, despite wanting to exact revenge for the senseless murder of those only following his commands. What very few knew though, For'son mused as he stood patiently in the entrance to the library, and he was one of the lucky ones, was that even as he stood speaking to Orac, plans had already been enacted that should, if they worked, provide some sort of flow of information by an underground network of dragons from within Ahrensburg, hopefully gaining them more insight and possibly even a chance of resolving the last remaining outpost to resist the opportunity to ally themselves with the rest of the planet and of course global peace. Unfortunately Orac was not in the loop at the moment.

"Does any of the evidence from our previous diplomatic attempts show anything but savagery and aggression?" asked the king's protector and friend.

"No, but it doesn't mean it's not there. Perhaps we're going about things all wrong. Just maybe in their culture, there's some sort of tradition when greeting outsiders for the first time and anything but that is an affront to them," suggested the librarian.

This gave For'son food for thought, admiring the guardian of the repository's stance and peace loving nature.

"I grant you that just maybe there is a chance that it's something like that, but don't you think it's more likely that their natural born dragon instincts are kicking in, urging them to fight rather than negotiate? If that's the case, then we have our backs to the wall if we want to bring them under our banner and show them a better way of life."

"What if they don't want the 'better' way of life that we're offering? Have you thought about what happens then?"

"I suppose it depends on who you're asking. Perhaps the leaders don't want change or peace... why would they if they can take what they want through violence, torture, intimidation and force? But the rest of the dragons there, struggling along, trying to make their way through life without rocking the boat or being noticed, subjugated and ruled through fear... what about all of them? And from what we know, that certainly seems to be the case."

"If that looks likely, then I understand the need to quite literally fight fire with fire. All I was pointing out is that there are many different ways to get to the same conclusion. Open your mind just a little, and you'll see that I'm right. You're in here all the time, reading tome after tome, devouring everything in front of you, which makes me not only very proud, but admire you even more. Take in some of the history stored on these shelves, learn lessons from times gone by, both good and bad, and you'll get a better sense of not only the world and the lands that it holds, but of yourself. I truly believe the knowledge held here can open up minds, inspire dragons not only to better themselves, but see reality in a much different way. In only a hundred or so years, think how much we've changed as a race, how we're more able and less violent. Now working together for the good of every single member of our kind, just the very thought of that would have been laughed at one hundred and fifty years ago, but look at what's been achieved. We're on the cusp of peace... who'd have ever thought that would have been possible?"

"It still might not be," voiced For'son, his concern about that very last land almost palpable across his huge prehistoric face.

"I don't think you believe that any more than I do," replied the librarian with a slight smile.

"I suppose not," answered the warrior.

"What say we agree to disagree and vow to try and look at any new differing situations from the others' point of view? Can't say fairer than that!"

"DONE!" replied For'son, playfully slapping Orac on the shoulder, much to the librarian's surprise.

"So what brings you to the darkest recesses of the city, For'son?"

"On my travels I found another... not quite library, more like a hole in the ground in which all of their scrolls were kept and what little reading material they possessed."

"Did you bring it back with you?"

"Sorry... no. It was all in quite a state and would almost certainly not have survived the journey. But I did read all that I could and would be honoured to recount it to you."

That sparked the fire of interest in the librarian's eyes.

"You're happy to do that?"

"I most certainly am," replied For'son, keen to get started.

"Now?"

"Sure."

And so grabbing two full bottles of ink, half a dozen quills and as much parchment as he could carry, Orac led the king's protector through the aisles of books to a massive table at the back of the underground space, before carefully clearing everything off it. After that, they both sat, the librarian unfurling the first of the blank scrolls.

Plummeting from the cold, dark sky, she landed with a bone rattling CRUNCH atop the soft, yellow sand of the beach, considering herself the luckiest dragon alive at having stumbled across landfall just in time. Unable to move even an inch, every muscle in her massive prehistoric body convulsed in fire-like agony, forcing her to cry out, something so undragon-like it made her head spin, so lost was she to the pain. As the howling gale continued to blow and the rain turned to a steady drizzle, the relatively young dragon, her golden, yellow and orange hues fitting right in with the surface she lay on, drifted off into unconsciousness, her very last thoughts centred on the mission she'd been tasked with. As the stark reality of failure hit her like the concussive force of a huge explosion, Keesha, as that was her name, apologised to the rest of her kin, not of course that they could hear her.

And so it was that the two started, For'son sitting motionless, eyes closed, his consciousness back in that

50

small dank room in the middle of the night, recalling everything he could, picking out each lazy swirl of the quill, making sure to get every last detail of not only the stories but the magic as well. It was important, he knew, to do it right and so very slowly and steadily the two of them proceeded to document all of it, with Orac patiently scribbling away as For'son forensically recalled all that he could.

By the end of the evening of the second day, they were close to finishing, having only stopped to quench their thirst and stave off the hunger in their rumbling bellies on a couple of occasions, and while the both of them held on tightly to their differing views and beliefs, they did, in this at least, work exceptionally well together.

Chance, that's all that it was, two well worn merchants cruising along the coastline as they always did, after which they'd cut inland taking the most direct route to the capital. About to veer off in a westerly direction to do just that, out of the corner of his left eye, one of the traders caught a glimmer of something golden sparkle in the fresh light of dawn in the now clear blue sky. Pulling up sharply, he immediately signalled his friend, not out loud, but using the familiar telepathic connection that nearly always remained open between the two of them.

"What is it?" the other asked, assuming that his constantly ravenous buddy had spied yet another woolly snack from a distance.

"There's something over there on the beach that warrants our attention."

"Are you sure?"

"I am. Quick, with me... let's investigate."

Following in his constantly hungry friend's wake, he banked sharply and wondered what had caught his keen eye.

Silently the dragons dropped to the seashore, both of

their huge feet making imprints almost a metre deep in the sand. Taking in the golden, yellow and orange dragon just lying there, it was the hungry one who spoke up first, this time out loud.

"We need to help her."

More than a little wary of the situation, mainly due to his age... nearly three hundred years, his partner could remember a time when a body out in the open like this would be used as part of an ambush, something his friend could see written across his face.

"It's not that... I'm sure. We live in a totally different world now. She needs our help."

Still more than a little unconvinced, reluctantly he agreed.

"Okay... check her out while I keep watch."

Without needing to be told twice, Doomos, the younger of the two by quite some way, bounded over to the splayed out dragon, knelt down and attempted to check for a pulse by placing his hand against the thin covering of golden yellow scales down her neck. Taking a deep breath, ignoring the breaking of the waves and the wind whistling in his ears, he closed his eyes and focused solely on his hand. After a moment or two, there it was, he was certain, a distinctive pulse, albeit a weak and unsteady one. Glancing over at his friend, he just had to let him know.

"She's alive, only barely though. What should we do?"

Considering their options whilst wondering what she was doing out here all alone and why she didn't have any gear with her, the more experienced of the two, Clondike, could only come up with one solution.

"We need to get her to the capital and fast."

"You mean carry her between us?"

"I do."

"Can we make it that far, with all our stuff as well?"

"With the storm having surrendered itself and with a stiffening wind heading in that direction, I think we could probably just about manage to carry her along with everything else. We do need to get a move on though."

And that was that, between the two of them, both fully loaded already with their supplies of herbs, spices and medicinal concoctions, they heaved her primeval body up into a standing position, their feet sinking even more into the sand, and on the count of three, both gave one huge flap of their wings, propelling them all skyward, after which they slowly came round and headed at pace towards the renowned dragon outpost of London.

Tapping into the source of all of their magic to keep them refreshed and focused, Orac and For'son had decided to plough on and finish the job that they'd started a couple of days ago now, with the librarian carefully cataloguing every word that his warrior partner recited, making sure that no mantra, spell or hex was either missed or misinterpreted.

With a palpable sense of relief washing off both of them, For'son recalled the last line of the final mantra, and letting out a long deep breath, dribbles of flame scorching the edge of both nostrils as he did so, he watched in satisfaction as the deft hand of the librarian finished the ultimate fancy swirl on the page. DONE! But no sooner had that happened than abruptly there was a familiar telepathic tickle, one he recognised from somewhere up above.

"For'son... what are you still doing down there?" asked the king with an edge in his voice.

"Recounting all of the tomes, spells, hexes, mantras and enchantments that I found during our last outing. We've just finished right now."

"You're with Orac?"

"I am."

"I need both of you up here, right now. We have something of an emergency."

"We're on our way sire," For'son replied, all businesslike, deep inside his head of course.

"Meet us in the medical section," the monarch ordered.

"Will do."

Starting to tidy away all his writing implements, abruptly Orac was grabbed by one of his tiny arms.

"We have to go... NOW... the king needs us, and before you ask, I don't know the details, only that it's an emergency."

Dropping the parchment and quills back on the table, the methodical librarian followed For'son's footsteps all the way to the access chute, and right in his wake dived off into the inky blackness, powering his wings as hard as he could in an effort to keep up.

Three minutes later, both of them rounded the corner of the tunnel that opened out into the fairly crude main medical section of the capital, to be greeted by the king standing there in all his prehistoric glory, conversing with the most senior of all the healers.

"Thank you. Please make sure to keep me apprised."

"Yes, sire."

"Ahh... just the dragons," sighed the monarch.

"Majesty," ventured Orac. "We came as quickly as we could."

"I don't doubt it," answered Greger, still looking a little... flustered, if ever a dragon king could be considered so.

"What's up?" asked For'son, not beating around the bush.

Turning ninety degrees, the king stretched out his wing and pointed in the direction of one of the huge beds hidden behind a gigantic glass screen. Following his lead, both dragons turned towards where he was indicating, to be greeted by a graceful golden dragon, with hints of orange and yellow dappled across the scales of her body.

"Wow!" reflected Orac, taken aback ever so slightly by her sheer beauty.

Greger gave him a look, one that told him just how inappropriate his comment had been.

"Sorry," he squeaked, much to For'son's amusement.

"That," started the king, "is something of a quandary."

"How so?" asked his warrior friend.

"She was brought in by those two merchants over there," stated the monarch, arching his head back to indicate the two dragons sitting on a stone bench right by the entrance. "They're traders and found this one lying on a beach off the east coast, with barely a pulse, hanging on for dear life."

"What's wrong with her?" observed Orac, hardly able to take his eyes off the golden dragon.

"They think it might be pure exhaustion," added the monarch.

"Hang on," interrupted For'son. "You're saying that she crossed the entire oceanic expanse in that storm... IMPOSSIBLE! It can't be done I tell you. Not in weather like that."

"How do you know what the weather was like out there?" asked Orac. "I've been with you consistently over the last couple of days. You haven't been outside."

Turning to face his friend, Greger was eager to hear his answer.

"There's a group of dragons that live just off the level one main plaza. More of a sort of hobby than anything business related, they've started to put together a kind of telepathic news bundle which they send out every day or so, sometime either late evening or early morning. It only contains any news that they can gather, which is quite sparse, and only really reaches those here in the capital, but the weather features all the time, and that's how I know, because I look out for their telepathic prompt."

"And you were reading that while we were still taking down all the information in the library?"

For'son nodded an affirmative.

"I think I'll have to keep my eye on this little group,"

reflected the king, squinting at his friend more than a little, which just looked odd given his huge prehistoric face. "Anyhow... ENOUGH! This is all very much a distraction from what I have to tell you."

Both dragons nodded and clamped shut their gigantic primeval jaws, ears pricked up.

"When she was brought in here, the doctor in charge heard her mutter one word and one word only."

"And just what was that?" enquired For'son of his friend.

All serious now, more so than anyone had seen him in a long time, the king gave a quick conspiratorial glance left and right, before whispering as quietly as he could.

"Ra-hoon!"

About to ask if either of them knew what it meant, the king's need to do so disappeared.

"Oh my," pondered Orac out loud.

"You know what it means," asked For'son, beating his friend to it.

The librarian just nodded his humungous head in reply.

"Well..."

Instantly recalling from his eidetic dragon memory what he'd read a very long time ago in a stash of burnt out books in a faraway land, the librarian took a few moments to compose himself before addressing both of those in front of him.

The deliberate silence felt less awkward and more filled with... suspense. Eventually Orac continued.

"They're creatures, rare and magical creatures."

That raised a couple of eyebrows, or it would have had the dragons had any, more of a concertina-ing of scales in a caterpillar effect above the eyes.

"And..."

"As dangerous as any of those I've ever read about or researched."

"You're kidding," piped up the king's protector.

"Noooooo," replied the librarian, clearly agitated.

"Tell us more," ordered Greger.

"They resemble a unicorn down to almost the very last detail."

"Those things wouldn't hurt a dragonling," For'son interrupted.

"Please... let me finish."

"Sorry."

"They resemble a unicorn almost down to the very last detail, apart from the fact that they have two horns instead of one."

That blew their minds. But before they could dwell on it, the guardian of everything written continued.

"Known to exist in the far away reaches of Southern Asia, Mongolia and China as we now know them, the black hearted cousins of the unicorns thrive in a dry, arid environment. As for their capabilities, well they mainly revolve around their mental prowess which easily allows them to assert their will over others, including dragons, maybe even controlling many at once. Rumours, and that's all they are as far as I remember, say that they can interrupt or even co-opt the telepathic communication of differing species, and not only do they feed physically as unicorns would, but they are also nourished by magic itself and often go in search of it."

The two dragons listening patiently really didn't like what they were hearing, or the obvious worry and concern with which Orac was delivering the news. And... it was only about to get worse.

"Some locals, it's been recorded, swear that they might even be able to use the magic of other races to power deadly mantras, spells and hexes. As well, and you're not going to want to hear this, but I'll say it anyway, for all intents and purposes they're invulnerable to just about any kind of magic. If ever a race could be considered apex predators, apart from us that is, it's this lot."

'Crikey,' thought For'son and the king simultaneously.

"Anything else?" asked the monarch.

"No... that's about it. But, as you've probably already worked out, they are extremely rare."

"That's at least something in our favour," mused the royal protector.

"But we need to know where this golden dragon has come from and why she's muttering that word," added the king.

"Can we wake her?" asked the librarian.

"Not at the moment... doing so now would present a clear and present threat to her life, is what I'm being told, that's how drained she is."

"I might have an answer to that," announced For'son, surprising both of the other two.

"Really?" exclaimed the king. "Do tell."

"There's a little known mantra that I've been working on in my spare time. I've been taking it apart because some of it is totally irrelevant, and splicing it with a couple of other lines of the supernatural. I would think it's absolutely perfect for this kind of situation."

"And it's safe?" ventured the king.

"As safe as any magic really gets."

"Ohh... that's inspiring. You want me to risk that young dragon's life on one of your absurd supernatural concoctions."

"It'll work. The only downside will be that it will leave me more than a little drained of mana. But I'll recover in a few days. Come on... what have you got to lose?"

'EVERYTHING,' thought Greger, but he didn't say it out loud.

And so with things appearing desperate, and with little choice in the matter, the king consented to let his friend try out his new spell out, it must be said very much against all the doctors' wishes.

Standing purposefully next to the bed the unconscious golden dragon lay on, still totally out of it, having told the others to remain behind the glass screen that separated her allocated sleeping area from everything else in the medical facility, For'son, more than a little nervous now with nearly a dozen dragons watching, took one, long, deep breath, swallowed in the hope of making his very dry mouth that little bit more moist, and closing his eyes, brought forth the words that he needed in the very front of his mind. Giving them the once-over to make sure they were totally and utterly correct, the courageous warrior dragon delved deep into his ethereal well of magic and in combination with his outstanding willpower, very casually shouted deep inside himself, focusing fully on the unconscious form before him.

Immediately the giant prehistoric head of the king's protector shot back as far as it would go, forcing him to look straight up at the grey stone ceiling, some fifty or so metres above him.

Behind the glass Orac, of all dragons, took two steps forward, preparing to intervene on For'son's behalf. An outstretched wing from the king stopped him dead in his tracks.

"Let it play out. I've no reason to doubt his courage, supernatural ability or intelligence. If he said it would work, we should trust that it will," mouthed the king.

The librarian dragon reluctantly shuffled back into place.

Beyond the window and between both the winged beings there, a light show like no other suddenly started taking place. Instantly particles of air ignited, twisted lines of volcanic red, cool cherry, toasted terracotta and soft vanilla filled the room, arcing out from For'son's gigantic primeval frame as he stood, eyes closed, chest puffed out.

Simultaneously, those watching all gasped at the event unfolding before them, aware of exactly what they were seeing. If you'd have asked humans to describe the colour they first thought of when either magic or mana was mentioned, almost certainly they would have picked blue. If you'd have asked a dragon, they would have said red, or at least some variation of it. They would have been right, and that's exactly what those looking on were seeing, the transfer of mana, or magic if you like, from one being to another, something at this time, tens of thousands of years ago, that had never happened before. For'son was nothing if not inventive, original and in supernatural circles, an innovator. Swirling, twirling, whirling around in the air, it didn't take long for the ethereal energy to find its intended target and home in on her, in one all out assault.

Abruptly, her muted gold, yellow and orange scales started to glow intensely as the multi-hued magic bombarded her motionless body. Out of nowhere, she let out a huge dragon sigh, licks of tiny flame backlighting her pristine white incisors, her dull pink tongue padding about trying to put them out, more through instinct than anything else. And then it happened. She opened her eyes and sat up, surprised to find herself in these surroundings.

As quickly as it was done, it was over, with Keesha, the golden dragon from a far off land, still taking in her whereabouts and the king's friend all but spent, having used up much of his ethereal energy. With For'son looking as though he would topple over, and knowing that the supernatural procedure had finished, Orac rushed around the side of the glass, and ignoring the beautiful golden dragon that he was so desperate to speak to, grabbed the royal protector, and guided him to a stone seat set back in the rock towards the top of the bed.

"Uhhh... thanks," uttered For'son, overcome with fatigue, his head spinning from using so much of his magic.

"Sit, sit," fussed Orac. "Stay there, I'll get you a drink."

It was only then that the librarian turned to face the exquisite looking female that now had her eyes on him.

"Hi..." was all that he could blurt out, that's how tongue tied he was.

"Hi yourself," replied the stunning looking dragon, stretching out her wings and raising her tiny little arms up over her head.

Not knowing what to say, having never spoken to a being so good looking and gorgeous before, it was then that the librarian was saved.

"Good afternoon, youngster,"

"Hello," was all that she could get out, as an imposing cranberry coloured dragon towered over not only her, but the tongue tied and shy dragon that had addressed her first of all. Wondering what was going on and exactly where she was, it didn't take long to find out.

"Don't worry... you're quite safe. You're in the capital... London! And in case you didn't know, I'm the dragon king... Greger."

For Keesha, it was a jaw-dropping moment. Meeting the reigning monarch... wow! It was more than she could have dreamed of when setting out all that time ago. And then it hit her, like a cold hammer pounding a hot forge.

"My... my... my kin sire, they're in trouble. That's why I'm here, to ask for assistance to deal with what's happening to us."

"Yes, yes my dear, we gathered as much. A problem with... the ra-hoon?"

"That's right. How did you know?"

"You mumbled it when you were brought in," added the librarian, suddenly finding his tongue, still very much in awe of the golden beast before him.

"Where are you from, and what seems to be going on?" asked the monarch, eager to get to the bottom of things.

And so with the king, Orac, and For'son albeit in quite a state, doubled over, holding his huge prehistoric head in his tiny little hands, all listening intently, the youngster tried to find the words to describe what had happened.

"My name is Keesha and I hail from the southern province of China, a thriving and peaceful land and one that's glad to be part of this new found, global dragon partnership that you've spearheaded, Majesty. Over the last decade things have been going well, with the underground tunnels linking us and the nearest cities nearly finished, agriculture flourishing, with peace and respect plentiful between all the dragons of our land. Three months ago, that all changed in the most dramatic of fashions. From out of nowhere, in the northern part of our territory, appeared a herd of beasts that we thought at first were unicorns. Boy, were we wrong!"

As Greger and the librarian listened patiently, the king's protector sat hunched over, rubbing his forehead, trying to clear the misty fog from his psyche, cutting through the clutter in an effort to hold onto the words that appeared, at least to him, to be coming from quite a distance away.

"Anyhow, we learned the hard way, losing half a dozen of our elders on that initial contact."

Unable to look either of the beings hovering over her in the eyes, getting more upset by the minute, Keesha dropped her head down to face the floor.

"They weren't killed or anything, far from it in fact. It might even have been better if they had been. Somehow the unicorn lookalikes had... I don't really know what to make of it. They'd taken over the minds of the dragon elders... all of them. Not only could you see it in their eyes, because they were almost totally white with no sign at all of an iris, but in their actions as well, which were vicious and beyond belief. To start with, the former elders would just raid our settlement and the few closest to it for food, ignoring anything else, not actually hurting anyone, but threatening to. All six together were intimidating to say the least, and so we just let them take what they wanted, it seemed better all round that way, and we thought that maybe they wouldn't come back. But they did, in even greater force, having somehow co-opted dragons from other settlements. And that's when it started... the real wickedness and evil. Not in their right minds, at least not from where we stood, the dragons not only steal our food now, but deliberately look for a fight, destroying everything and every being in their path. Perfectly innocent dragons have been killed, ambushed in the most heinous of ways, for no apparent reason. And as if this weren't bad enough, they went after our nursery ring last week, killing three youngsters before enough of us could get there to defend them."

Recounting this part caused Keesha's hands to shake and her eyes to fill up, barely able to continue, but she did, because she knew how important it was to those of her kind back home, despite her voice wobbling precariously.

"We don't know how to defeat these ra-hoon creatures and have tried everything at our disposal. On occasion some of our warriors have got close enough to attack them with magic, albeit from some height, all to no avail. Nothing supernatural, as far as we know, can hurt them. And to say that they're smug when all this happens is something of an understatement."

Forcing her beautifully scaled golden face to look up, she gazed directly into Greger's eyes, holding her stare, despite the flow of teardrops down her primeval cheeks.

"Please, Majesty, will you help us? We don't know what to do, and just long to tend our land and live out the rest of our lives in peace and quiet."

Opening his huge jaws, about to speak, a voice from off to one side beat him to it.

"We'll most certainly help," commented For'son, still clearly suffering the effects of transferring a fair deal of his magic over to the graceful golden dragon. "It's been a while since I've had a real challenge, and this sounds like it could very much be the next one."

"Are you up to the task?" asked his friend the king, concerned at just how drained he looked.

"It'll be okay," sighed the warrior, before turning to address their guest. "How long did it take you to get here?"

"Four days," she replied.

Impressive, all three of them thought at once.

"Was that non-stop?" asked Orac, amazed that any being could cover that distance in such a short space of time.

"Nearly," replied Keesha. "I slept for about an hour a day, and if not for that brutal storm front last night, then I would have been here much sooner. By the way, how did I get here? I can remember stumbling across solid ground and crashing into some sand, after that though, it's all a bit of a mess."

"The two merchants over there," observed the king, pointing out past the glass screen with the tip of his right wing, "found you in bad shape lying on the beach. Much to their credit, they brought you straight here, which probably saved your life, youngster. I should thank them when you get the chance."

"I will do, sire."

It was then that things got back to business.

"What is it you need, For'son?" declared the monarch.

Turning towards the beautiful and entrancing golden dragon, the king's protector asked the obvious question.

"How many ra-hoon are there? You said a herd, how many does that mean?"

"We've counted seven in all, but with the way they seem to work, one would probably cause us trouble enough."

Standing up, still a little unsteady on his feet, the warrior pondered what he was up against. Deciding not to take a huge force because it just didn't seem necessary, particularly given the distance involved, he opted to go with a familiar solution.

"I'll go back with Keesha and if I need support I'll enlist some of the locals to help out."

"Are you sure?" asked Greger.

"It'll be alright, and let's face it, it's not like it's the first time. Like it or not, these ra-hoon creatures are going down."

"Ummm... are you seriously sending just him to help out?" ventured their guest, hardly able to believe what she was hearing.

"I can understand how you might have concerns, but don't worry, he's the best of the best, and the reason you're feeling so good right at this moment. Five minutes ago, you were still unconscious and at least days away from waking. I assure you, you'll be in safe hands in his company," replied the king, very much aware that Orac was hopping about like a squirrel whose nuts had got trapped in a vice.

"What is it?" demanded the king, turning to address the repository guardian who seemed entirely unable to stand still.

"L... l... let me go with them," was all that he could stutter, convinced he could be of some help.

That provoked a rip-roaring riposte of laughter from For'son, at just the very thought of the librarian accompanying them.

"W... w... what's so funny?" uttered Orac, more than a little overwhelmed at the situation he found himself in.

"YOU... out of the library, in the real world, dealing with dangerous magical beasts... it's hard to picture in my head," the king's protector responded.

"I can be of use... I know I can. Please..." said the librarian, addressing Greger directly, "I can do this, and be of help, I'm sure of it."

"Hmmm..." growled the king against the background rumble of his huge scaled belly. "I'm not quite as convinced as I usually would be, but I suppose your knowledge might come in useful. FOR'SON," he went on, turning to face his friend. "Take Orac with you, if for no other reason than to grant him some experience. And keep him safe, I'm entrusting his life to you... understood?"

About to argue against such action, out of the corner of his left eye he could see just how desperate the librarian was to join their cause, and so instead of objecting he just swallowed, his throat feeling as dry as the Sahara desert, and nodded an affirmative. It wasn't ideal he knew, bringing someone along who had absolutely no fighting experience, but what he lacked in physicality and offensive magic, he more than made up for in intelligence. Perhaps the king was right and his expertise might provide a solution in that far away state.

And so with that decided, six hours later, and after having said their goodbyes to the king, the three of them found themselves perched precariously on the outer battlements of the capital, London, looking out across the meandering river, their stomachs filled and their bags packed, about ready to launch into the air.

"Are you sure you want to do this?" Forson asked Orac, one last time.

"Nodding eagerly, the considerably smaller prehistoric monster offered a thumbs up with both of his spindly hands.

"Let's do this then," suggested the warrior who, while not fully recovered from his earlier magical exertions, was well on his way to being fully fit. "Would you like to lead the way?" he said, addressing Keesha who looked utterly magnificent in the moonlight.

Smiling, she gave him a nod, before turning back towards the horizon, and bounding off the battlement. Noting the thrill on the librarian's face, For'son indicated with just the shake of his head that Orac should follow. Visibly gulping before he threw himself into the air, the shy and retiring librarian grinned from ear to ear, nodding in the warrior's direction. Shaking his head, wondering what he'd got himself mixed up in this time, the king's courageous protector leapt skywards, and with two flaps of his powerful wings, found himself trailing in their wake, only the cold, dark blanket of the night sky for company.

"Sire, sire, sire," cried out Walker, one of the king's military commanders and a dragon who, surprisingly, didn't like to fly, hence his given name.

"Yes, what is it now? I'm in the middle of assessing the

plans for the new subterranean geothermal power producing plant."

"I'm sorry, Your Majesty, but I really don't think this can wait."

"Okay... come on in. What is it that's so important?"

"We've just had word from... Ahrensburg!"

That would have knocked the king's socks off, had he been wearing any. Imagine it... dragon socks, that would be one outlandish knitting project.

"Explain!" ordered Greger.

"For some time we've covertly been trying to cultivate contacts within Ahrensburg's borders, up until now with little success, the fear of retribution from their leader all encompassing, with absolutely no one willing to help out. Two weeks ago a dragon approached us by one of the back channel means that we nearly always have open, telling us that he wanted to help. I won't tell you his name for security reasons, but this is from him, for your eyes only."

"Okay," said the king, grabbing the grubby looking, folded up piece of parchment that had been sealed on one side with some runny brown wax.

Opening it carefully, wondering if it might be a trap of some sort, but not really seeing how, slowly, he read the words, all the time shaking his huge dinosaur-like head from side to side.

"Everything alright, Majesty?" asked Walker, wondering what the message might be.

Finishing up, and noting the commander's interest, the monarch handed over the parchment to his subordinate.

"They want to establish diplomatic contact," Walker mused incredulously.

"So it would seem, so it would seem."

"But that's... absolutely unheard of. Over the course of five hundred years they've continued to spurn our overtures of peace and good relations. All we've ever heard coming out of there are tales of torture, violence, subjugation and terror. And suddenly they want to do it by the book, potentially be friends. I don't buy it... not one bit."

"I grant you, it does seem odd. Perhaps though they heard about our latest conquest and are only now realising that it's our way or the highway. That wouldn't be much of a surprise."

"It would be to me. That Nev'dir is one hell of a psychopath, and that's just from what we know. The way he treats those under him is disgraceful. Murder, rape, torture are some of the tools in the arsenal he regularly uses against his own kin, and that's just to start with. They all live in fear of what he will do next, none willing to stand up to him and his lieutenants."

"I understand what you're saying," reflected the king, "but if there really is an opportunity to broker a diplomatic solution, we can't afford to miss out on it. This could very well be our one and only chance to bring the whole of the world together, every last dragon under one banner. No more fighting, no more arguing, bickering, all of us getting on together, making the planet a better place, not just for those in charge, but all dragonkind. It's what I've dreamed of for decades now and I can almost touch it, that's how tangible it is."

"I know you're passionate about this, sire, and not only do I understand, but I share your sentiment," replied Walker, doing his best to try and balance the conversation. "But this dragon is dangerous, more so than any other we've come up against... EVER! Don't be lulled into a false sense of security, don't lower your guard, and don't, under any circumstances, take his word on anything."

"As always, I appreciate your counsel my friend and I know what you say makes a great amount of sense, so I'll think carefully about how to proceed. I would suggest you do the same. In the meantime, I would like you to get a message back to your contact inside Ahrensburg, saying that we're open to diplomatic dialogue and would like to progress things further."

"Understood, sire. It'll take a few days to get it there, but I'll make sure it's done and that we watch out for any response."

"Thank you. Dismissed."

And with that, Walker turned on his talons and marched straight out of the room, leaving the monarch alone with his thoughts.

'Can I do it? Is it really possible to unite the whole of the planet and bring dragonkind together? We've been so close for so long, perhaps this is the stroke of luck we need to get us over the line,' Greger reflected, lost in dreams of victory parades and statues in his honour, wanting nothing more than to spread peace around the globe. Would it, could it, be that easy? It was doubtful to say the least, but he had to at least try. But with the potential for treachery and double dealing, he'd have to think carefully about who to put in charge. Of course he had a diplomatic corps full of qualified dragons, but none who inspired the kind of confidence he was looking for in something this sensitive and important. Perhaps sending a being more worldly wise would be the best way to resolve something like this. 'Oh well,' he mused, knowing that at least for now, time was on his side.

Sheltering out of the midday sun beneath a rocky bluff, all seven ra-hoon feasted like there was no tomorrow, as was their wont, gobbling and slurping nearly all of the meat, fruit and vegetables that the dragons they now controlled had stolen on their behalf. Of course they knew to save a little back to keep their minions, as that's how they regarded them, just fit enough to fight, not having to worry about any treachery because their mental influence was all encompassing, with no creature in their history having developed a strategy to either resist or escape. It simply wasn't possible, not even for these winged beasts who considered themselves not only masters of the sky, but of the ground as well. That, they all thought, was about to change... BIG TIME!

Soaking up the radiant rays of the sun, warming themselves atop shiny orange and yellow rocks, their magic regulating the temperatures within their prehistoric bodies, two dozen dragons sprawled out a short way away from their masters... the ra-hoon, were unable to comprehend their previous lives or remember even a snippet about their friends. Not so much lost as tempered by the imperious will of the cunning and deceitful beasts that they now served, any recollection of family was suppressed one hundred percent. And so, knowing nothing else, they marinated themselves in the heat, postured, fought over what little food was thrown their way, all the time readying themselves for the next bout of action. Simply existing, their lives could in no way be described as living, not as they'd previously known. Little did they know that their masters were planning an all out, gung-ho, for them at least, attack, determined to subjugate the remaining dragons within all the settlements they'd been stalking for months in an effort to form their own dragon army. Grandiose hopes and dreams were shared across the ra-hoon link nearly constantly, whether night or day.

Forty eight hours into their flight, the three, not so much friends, more like... polite acquaintances, dropped out of the sky onto a small tree lined isle in the midst of a quiet and tranquil turquoise sea.

The very first thing For'son did on landing was wade waist high into the sea, splashing the warm foamy water all over his weary body, enjoying every second of it, almost visibly washing away the aches and pains. Watching from the shore, amazed that he would do such a thing, at least with anyone else around, it didn't take long for his two comrades to join him for a soak, even Orac who was tentative to say the least. But once in, they didn't hold back on the frolicking around. After an hour or so, they all reluctantly left the water, allowing themselves to be dried off by the last of the sun's rays, For'son ordering the other two to chop down some trees and make a fire, while he found them some food. And boy... did he! Two sweeping circumferences of the isle and he'd found exactly what he was looking for, and in two separate journeys back to where they'd made their camp, much to Keesha and the librarian's surprise, he arrived with two fully grown cows and three mature sheep, all of which had been put out of their misery in the most considerate and humane way (that's an odd choice of words given that humans at this time could only be regarded as cavemen), if such a thing were at all possible.

And so they ate, and talked very little, which suited all of them for different reasons. Orac because he was so shy, For'son because of his professionalism, fully focused now on what needed to be done once they arrived at their destination, and Keesha because she was in the presence of relative strangers and didn't really know what to make of the other two. After that they slept for a couple of hours, having made good time so far, with the jet stream having been very much on their side. Whether it would remain that way was anyone's guess.

Awoken by his supernatural gift, exactly on time, For'son roused his companions, and once refreshed from splashing some seawater on to their faces, they bounded into the cool night air, continuing with their important mission.

Thirty two hours later, the three comrades in arms, led by Keesha, buffeted by warm, dry air, dropped from the sky on to a peach coloured plateau, wings burning from the brutal journey that they'd just undertaken. Relieved to have arrived, the two males followed the young female's lead.

"This way," Keesha announced, tramping off in the direction of a huge cave entrance only a hundred or so metres away.

For'son and Orac followed on behind, neither saying very much, both utterly exhausted from their long flight.

On reaching the cave's entrance, the golden hued dragon turned around, clearly looking for something.

"What is it?" asked For'son, his sharp mind picking up that something was wrong.

"My kind should be here in great numbers, and yet there seems to be no one about. As well, I can't get a sense of any of them telepathically, so they're not even close by."

"That doesn't bode well," added the librarian, nervously.

"Fall in behind me," ordered the warrior of the three, knowing that they were now very much in danger, which, given their current state was not ideal to say the least.

"What do we do now?" said Orac.

"We could make camp inside the cave and wait for them to come back," suggested Keesha, "there's bound to be supplies and bedding, and I'm sure the others won't mind us using it temporarily."

"NO!" stated For'son, having already assessed the situation.

"But..."

Turning to face the youngster, his magical senses already extended out as far as they would go, on the lookout for anything remotely unusual, he calmed himself and tried to put on a brave front for the other two, despite not really wanting to.

"We can't go into the cave, because... if we do, and they come back under the ra-hoon's spell, we'll be trapped and then it'll all be over. I understand your thinking, but we have to stay out in the open, so that we can at least retreat into the air if we have to."

"O... o... o... okay," she replied, her mind spinning at

the realisation that her friends and family might have fallen victim to the unicorn doubles' dastardly dealings.

"I'm sorry," resumed the warrior, "But I think we have to assume that they've been taken by the ra-hoon in the same way the others have."

Nodding her understanding, Keesha bravely fought back the tears, determined not to show exactly how upset she was. It was then that it came to her.

"There's a ridge further up the valley, one that provides good cover, easy access to the air, and best of all, looks down on the area where those monsters normally hang out."

"Great!" exclaimed the king's protector. "Show us where to go and we'll follow. Perhaps skirt around the back of the ridge if at all possible. We don't want to go anywhere near the ra-hoon's position because we don't know the range of their powers. And now they have more fighters, travelling around will be much more difficult. Stay well away from other dragons, even if you think that you know them. If they're enchanted or under some sort of spell, they'll report us immediately and that would be a disaster."

"I understand," replied Keesha. "There's a little known back route that most don't use because of the dangerous updrafts. Do you want to try that?"

"That sounds best. I know you're both exhausted, and so am I, but we have to find somewhere safe to put down before we can rest. Hopefully this will be our last flight for a while. Good work so far... both of you." With one brilliant blue shimmering wing, For'son indicated to the stunning looking female that she should take to the air. "Lead the way."

Traversing the rear of the ridge which involved flying against what felt like a storm front over a thousand metre drop off, eventually, after both Keesha and For'son had saved Orac from being splattered against the sharp, jagged rocks on at least two occasions each, the three of them touched down on top of a much smoother and more concealed table, edged by mountainous boulders and sharp, uneven rocks, gaps in which looked out across the valley below, giving a view superseded by no other.

"Follow me," whispered Keesha. "There's an overhang up here that will provide cover from the air, but won't box us in. There are also gaps through which we should be able to view what's going on down below."

And so they did, surprised at what they found. It was exactly as she'd said, secluded, with enough space for the three of them, and plenty of little lookouts to view the valley below. Of course it might be tricky during the night. Even the tiniest lick of flames would stand out through the holes, giving away their position to the enemy, something For'son had been thinking about for a while now.

'If they had a couple of dozen dragons before, just how many do they have now?' he wondered. From what Keesha had already told him, the missing dragon villagers numbered in their dozens, maybe as many as sixty in all. If the vast majority of those had unwittingly allied themselves with the ra-hoon, then he'd probably bitten off more than he could chew, an unusual occurrence for any dragon, least of all him.

Sitting in a line, plumping to perch on the cool, sand covered rock, carefully they pressed their huge prehistoric heads up against the gaps in the stone that they'd each selected and, adjusting their vision to what could be regarded as 'telescopic', they all scanned the valley below for any sign of their enemy the ra-hoon and the missing villagers. It didn't take long to find what they were seeking.

Having already agreed to use their telepathic powers to communicate, not knowing how far their voices would travel across the range they found themselves hidden in, it was the golden, yellow and orange female that broke the silence of their psyches first.

"I can see all the villagers out beyond the bluff at the far end of the valley. They're grouped with those that had already been taken. I think we can assume that they've all gone the same way."

"What are they all doing?" Orac's voice whispered across the link, much to For'son's amusement.

"Lying about, soaking up the sun," Keesha replied.

"Hmmm..." echoed the warrior's voice throughout all of their minds.

"What is it?" enquired the librarian, still more than a little out of his depth in the real world, on a mission.

"I've found the ra-hoon, about two hundred wingspans this side of the dragons, just milling about in a large group. How far away would you say that we are Orac?"

"About a thousand wingspans, maybe even more."

"And they haven't cottoned on that we're here and we haven't had our minds invaded by them?"

"No."

"It was rhetorical."

"Sorry."

"No problem."

"What are you thinking?" asked Keesha.

"Just wondering about the range of their abilities. It would be interesting to know just how close we can get without being affected."

"I might be able to help with that," piped up Orac, giving them both a knowing smile.

"And...?"

"Throughout much of our exhausting journey here, I scoured my memory for anything useful that we could use against the unicorn lookalikes."

"Yes..." said the graceful female, fluttering her eyelashes, urging him on.

"It is possible, from what I can gather, to build a defensive shield around a dragon's mind."

"WHAT?!" exclaimed For'son, having never heard anything like it in all his travels and library visits.

Continuing despite his comrade's rude interruption, Orac felt as alive as he ever had on catching the scent of the beautiful Gold as he thought of her.

"On three separate occasions it's been noted down that dragons have tried this with varying success."

"That's not doing it then, is it, especially if they've failed spectacularly."

"All three attempts didn't fail, only two... the other, well... let's just say she did an outstanding job of thinking outside the box."

"Really?"

"Pretty much."

"And you have the mantra that she used?"

"I do." With that, Orac pulled a folded up piece of parchment out of the humungous pocket lining his belly that all dragons have, some more so than others (no names... shopkeeper) and handed it across to his crystalline blue friend.

In total and utter silence, with the other two watching on, For'son studied the words in front of him, having never seen anything like it. It was then that the librarian spoke up.

"This is exactly what we're doing back in London, the whole point of the library... to uncover valuable magic like this, to use for the good of our kind."

'He's right,' thought the warrior, agreeing totally with the sentiment. But to use a mantra that hadn't been tried and tested was risky beyond belief, especially something that looked so old, and something all of his battle hardened senses shied away from immediately.

"The book it's taken from tells the tale of a settlement fighting off three deadly dark dragons that had adapted their telepathic talents to instead invade minds, corrupting all those they touched, killing some immediately, forcing other psyches to implode leaving their bodies husks of what they once were, unable to feed, fight or even stand. With half of their encampment decimated, the brightest minds left got together under cover of dark in an effort to pool their intelligence and magic to put an end to the evil casting a shadow over all of them. What you have in front of you is the result of their knowhow and toil."

"So you say, but will it work?"

"Well," whispered the librarian, *"why don't we test it out?"*

'Wow,' thought Keesha, 'this has gone from bad to worse,' knowing full well that testing ancient and unusual mantras had the potential to go very, very badly. 'Oh well, in for a penny, in for a pound.'

"What would you have us do Orac?"

"Use the mantra, and Keesha and I will try and use our telepathy to attack your mind... in the friendliest way possible."

It did kind of make sense, For'son begrudgingly told himself, and the goal was a worthy one, because if the spell did work, it would prove to be a huge advantage in righting the ra-hoon's huge wrong. But it was still a very big IF, as far as he was concerned.

"Okay... we'll give it a try, but go gentle while we're still testing it... right?"

"Sure," they both mouthed simultaneously, much to their amusement.

Away from the hole in the rock now, with absolutely no possibility of anyone down below spotting them, the courageous and talented warrior dragon closed his huge dinner plate sized eyes, took a few deep breaths, and brought forth the words at the front of his mind, clearing his thoughts of anything else.

Written in an exceptionally ancient tongue, he did understand most of it, but not all. But that didn't matter, not so long as he applied enough magic and a considerable amount of his powerful will. Ready... he did just that.

Instantly, he felt different, but it was difficult to tell why. And then he had something. He couldn't feel either of the others, well... not with his eyes closed. Before, he could sense their presence, mentally anyhow, but not now. There was nothing, just the bare rock, the sand grating on his talons and the air surrounding him. He knew they were both there next to him, he could hear their breathing for goodness sake, but for all intents and purposes they were invisible to his mind. Only then did he decide to try and retreat inside himself to see what he could find. Pulling back, barely breathing at all, which didn't really matter that much as dragons can hold their breath for round about an hour if they have to, handy when diving beneath water in the hunt for elusive fish in faraway places, he continued his search.

Feeling not only in control, but experiencing a certain sense of familiarity, instantly he recognised where he was, well... kind of. In a mixture of whites, greys and blacks, words and sentences were cut into the wall of wherever it was his intellect currently resided. It took a few moments before he got it, but when he did, he was utterly astounded.

'The writing... that's everything my eidetic memory has ever come across.'

And he was right... it was. Within something resembling half a sphere, words and sentences zipped about in mid-air, some of them mantras, others chit-chat, the occasional pivotal moment in there as well. Abruptly, the walls and writing faded, still visible... just, more translucent than anything, revealing a layered outer wall beyond, like that of an igloo, forming a strong outer casing to his mind, all but impenetrable, or at least that was the hope.

Back in reality, Orac was... frustrated, having already tried half a dozen times to breach the mental defences of the dragon he admired the most. Alright, he gave him a hard time about how he handled himself, but inside he did at least recognise the need for For'son's unique skill set, the passion and dedication with which he protected the king and his keen grasp of all things written and magical, as well as his propensity to seek out new knowledge in an effort to expand his mind. That one thought gave him an idea about a new approach to the test that they were running. If he couldn't break in, perhaps he could lure the warrior's mind out.

Sitting beside the two of them, Keesha had followed

Orac's instructions to the letter, gently prodding and probing the mental part of the bright, blue dragon only a few metres away, hoping to get some kind of response or feel his intellect on a basic level. Surprisingly though, it was hidden away, buried for all intents and purposes, impossible to get hold of, however hard she tried, and she did, only now giving all that she had in an effort to do so, but to no avail.

Still studying the inside of his mind, mouth open, well... it would have been, gaping in fact, in awe at his surroundings, only then did he feel a pressing need to ... what? A vaguely familiar tug in the right direction suddenly made him feel... alive, with a tangible buzz making his silent and still body tingle all over. Without him knowing it, his brain chemistry started to change, lighting up neurons inside his head, pulling his attention in a different direction to where it had previously been.

'Knowledge,' he thought... 'somewhere out there is undiscovered information that I just have to get my hands on.' If he'd applied a little logic to the situation, he'd have realised quite quickly the impossibility of it all, sitting as he was with his two cohorts beneath a rocky overhang at the top of a ridge in the middle of what was essentially a desert. But he didn't, or more accurately... couldn't, because his all encompassing addiction had him in its grasp. That's right, he was addicted... to finding knowledge, especially the magical kind. Wherever he went across the world on the king's orders, he sought out anything he could that was supernatural and written down, not for his own purposes of course, but to help ensure its survival by bringing it back to the library in London, having it copied for future generations to see and use as they would see fit. Here and now though, his compulsion had him scrabbling about in an effort to lower his defences so that he could get out and get his hands, I mean mind, on that sumptuous information that he just couldn't resist, something the librarian was counting upon.

"It's no use," declared Keesha to Orac, *"no matter how hard I try, I simply cannot touch him."*

"That's good my dear," replied the librarian, *"it means that the mantra is working. I however have a little plan in motion, something that any second now should come to fruition."*

And it did... right there and then!

Nothing else existed, not in that moment, so bad was his craving for the lost knowledge that he was sure was out there. And so he did the one thing that he shouldn't, the one thing that, if he were truly facing the ra-hoon, would cost him his life and bring about a resounding defeat. He dismissed the mantra he'd cast, the one that Orac had given him, and returned to reality in search of the information that he thought was out there spurred on by his infatuation.

"Gotcha!" screamed the librarian across the telepathic boundaries of their link, the moment For'son lowered his defences.

'DAMN!' thought the warrior, coming back to his senses, knowing full well that not only had he been caught out, but he'd been played as well, the ramifications of which did not bode well for any encounter with the monstrous beasts down below in the valley.

"Did it work?" asked Keesha trying to break the ice between the other two and change the subject slightly.

"To some degree it did," ventured the warrior, still smarting from being caught out by the repository guardian.

"Until I lured you out," added Orac, a little too smugly.

"Hmmm..."

"Surely that's something though, isn't it?" commented the sparkling golden female in their midst.

"It is," answered For'son, feeling more than a little downcast, something the librarian quickly picked up on.

"Don't take it personally," Orac quipped. *"I only managed to catch you out because I knew your Achilles heel... your passion for seeking out undiscovered knowledge. Without that, I would have had nothing and no way to draw you into the open. The ra-hoon don't*

know that, and so they wouldn't have been able to succeed."

Although true, it felt like a small crumb of comfort to the brilliant blue shaded warrior who very much felt as though he'd failed.

"Right at the start, we both probed and prodded with all the magic that we had to try and break through to your mind," noted the librarian. *"To say we failed spectacularly would be something of an understatement. How did it feel for you?"*

Trying to take the positives from their little experiment, For'son considered his answer.

"My mind felt as though it was walled off, that's the only way I can explain it. But it worked both ways. With my eyes closed, while my intelligence felt safe and free from any attack, I couldn't sense either of you, despite the fact that I knew you were there and could hear your breathing."

"Excellent!" exclaimed the repository's guardian. *"It means that the mantra worked and protected your mind. If it can do that, it should be able to keep the ra-hoon at bay, at least long enough for us to take them down."*

That did seem like a positive, the warrior supposed, but there was one problem that currently they'd overlooked, not so much an elephant in the room but a multitude of dragons. And what would that be, I hear you ask?

The captured kin of Keesha, who all currently remained under the spell of the dastardly unicorn lookalikes, because to get to the ra-hoon, almost certainly they'd have to go through those first.

"You're thinking about the villagers," the young female announced, more of a statement than a question.

"Some immunity to the mental acuity of the ra-hoon is welcome, but I don't doubt for one second they'll throw the whole lot at us, before I can get anywhere even vaguely close to them. And that's going to be a problem."

"I don't want them harmed," Keesha contemplated out loud, *"but, if there's truly no other way, then it must be done. Under no circumstances should those monsters be allowed to co-opt any more beings. If it takes the lives of those that I regard as friends and family*

to do just that, then I say to you now, knowing each and every one of them, that's what they would want you to do."

It was heartbreaking to hear her speak like that... not only so casually, but callously as well. No dragon so young should have to make decisions with such consequences.

"What if we could draw them away?" suggested Orac.

"Go on," urged For'son.

"Keesha and I could draw the dragon contingent away somewhere, giving you the chance to attack the ra-hoon themselves, ably protected by the mantra you've just tried out."

"Hmmm... it might work."

"D... d... d... do you think there's a chance that my kin might come back after the beasts that have done this are slain?"

For'son nodded at the librarian, urging him to answer the question, knowing that he understood what was involved a little more and would therefore be able to make a better judgement.

"I can't say for certain, but my best guess would be an optimistic yes. I can't think for one minute that the minds and personalities of those under the control of the unicorn lookalikes have been wiped, only suppressed. If that's the case, and it is a big IF, then I would surmise that if the ra-hoon are eliminated, then things should return to normal. It is only a guess though."

"Based on all the evidence and experience that you have," added the warrior.

"Yes."

Keesha nodded in thanks, pleased they'd been honest with her and not just come out and said what they thought she wanted to hear.

"What do we do now?" asked the dazzling female, laying her head back next to the peach coloured rock she was sitting against.

For'son took that one.

"We make a plan for the morning."

As night fell and the twinkling stars started to reveal themselves, the three of them curled up beneath the secluded rocky overhang, high up on the perilous ridge that overlooked the valley, discussing battle tactics, attempting to find the perfect way to separate the ra-hoon from the dragons.

On the valley floor, the white, grey and brown unicorn lookalikes, with two horns instead of the usual one, had curled up between a series of twenty metre tall rocks, all asleep, occasionally whinnying, their powerful magic still maintaining a grip on the dragons under them who were only a hundred or so metres away, themselves asleep, their snoring resembling that of a congested hippo, all but empty husks of their former selves.

With an almighty yawn, accompanied by licks of searing orange and yellow flame from around the edges of his mouth and his huge scaled nostrils, Greger watched the slow trickle of thick gelatinous lava that slowly worked its way beneath his office floor, designed to heat and light up the room, all the time trying to shake off the fatigue that he felt from having very little sleep over the last couple of days, concern for his friends off in a faraway land partly to blame, worry about the Ahrensburg situation only compounding things further.

Abruptly a knock on the door startled him from his far flung thoughts.

"COME," he said, a little more harshly than he'd meant to.

In strolled Walker, a piece of parchment flapping about in one of his tiny hands.

"Sire," he said, bowing his huge brown prehistoric head as he did so.

"Walker," replied the king. "What do you have?"

"They've replied, Majesty."

"And?"

"It's good news. They're willing to host a diplomatic

delegation with a view to discussing the cessation of hostilities."

Those words, not only lifted a huge weight off Greger's shoulders, but put a gigantic smile across his scaled face.

"Do they have some sort of timeframe?"

"Three weeks."

"Wow... that's pretty soon. Is there any kind of wriggle room?"

"No. They were quite specific in their reply... here, see for yourself," ventured Walker, handing the king the parchment.

Taking a few moments to read what was in front of him, the monarch lost his previously gained smile, becoming more serious with every line that he read.

"So," he stated, more than a little annoyed, "it's either in three weeks or not at all? Doesn't that strike you as a little odd?"

"A little, but perhaps it's just one of their customs that we don't know about. They seem to have many intricacies, from what little we do know."

"Hmmm..." mouthed Greger, more than a little sceptical and unimpressed.

"It all seems... a little too good to be true, don't you think Walker?"

"I know what you're saying, but we've done things the right way, and our contact, I'm assured, is one hundred percent reliable."

"Okay... we'll take it on good faith at the moment. Round up a diplomatic team and start getting them as prepared as possible. I want them ready to move in exactly three weeks. We'll give them what they want."

"Okay sire. Who should I choose to lead the delegation?"

"I'll be choosing the leader," observed the king, "and he won't be a diplomat. Just gather up the rest of what's needed and keep it small. I want as few dragons as possible going."

"Understood," answered Walker, bowing before turning and leaving, wondering who the hell would lead the delegation and why any number of the top diplomats hadn't been selected for the job. Clearly, he thought, the king had other ideas.

And the king did, with one individual specifically in mind for the role.

Squinting across the horizon, warming the coolness of the desert, the sun lighting up their little pocket of shelter was enough to wake them all at about the same time. With the exception of telepathic *"good mornings"*, the first thing that For'son, Orac and Keesha did was to cautiously look out through the gaps in the rock nearest to them, down into the valley below, eager to see whether or not their opponents were still asleep. They were, the dragons' snores resembling a combine harvester in a field full of glass.

"Are you ready" For'son asked, laying his pack on the floor, knowing that whatever the outcome, he wouldn't need it for the time being.

"Yes," they replied simultaneously, each looking more than a bit sheepish.

"It'll be okay as long as you don't deviate from the plan. Draw the dragons out, as many as you can, and lead them on the wildest goose chase possible. You already know the places where you can lose them... so Orac, follow her lead. If she gives you an instruction, do it as if your life depends on it... it probably will. Okay?"

Two nods later, and they were ready to go.

"Good luck," voiced For'son, telepathically.

"To us all," added Keesha.

And with that they were done, the warrior disappearing off towards the exit, before leaping over the massive drop off at the rear of the ridge, as the other two prepared themselves.

"Remember," whispered the gorgeous golden female through their link, *"we don't want to hurt any of the dragons. We*

just need to buy your friend some time."

"*Understood,*" replied the librarian, suddenly thinking of For'son as his friend. Was he? He supposed so, but when did that happen? It was almost as if it had sneaked up on him. Unable to remember a time when he'd had a true friend, briefly it made his heart warm at just the very thought. But there was no time to dwell on it, not here and not now, because right at this very moment, it was time to act. Following the beguiling female dragon out of the overhang, darkened clear blue sky above getting brighter by the second, as she leapt upwards he followed her lead, very much hoping that he would be reunited with his pal at the end of all this.

Negotiating the wild and unpredictable currents and updrafts using all his worldly experience, almost getting slammed into the sheer cliffs twice from some unfavourable crosswinds, the king's protector had successfully skirted the back of the huge ridge that rose up above the gorge they had sheltered on top of, and had turned back and entered the southern part of the valley, now gliding effortlessly low to the ground in total and utter silence, his menacing presence casting a shadow beneath him onto the hard, chilly ground, causing rodents, birds and insects to scatter in all directions, the blazing blue of his scales glinting in the dappled rays of first light. Abruptly he pulled up, spreading his mighty wings vertically, using them as air brakes, drawing to a halt on a rocky crest that was almost an island in an oasis of sand. From here he had the perfect view of his prey, the rahoon, not quite stirring, unable to shake off their previous night's indulgences, and by that I mean all of the food stolen from the surrounding villages that they'd consumed. Mental fortifications already in place thanks to Orac's mantra, he hoped he'd get the chance to add that to the London library which the two of them were very slowly developing. And then it hit him, in the same way it had Orac only a short while ago... they'd become firm friends over the course of their time spent arguing during all those late nights in the library. There and then, he made a vow to tell him once they'd gotten over all this, though that wasn't straightforward by any means. Hunched down as close to the surface of the rocky crest as his massive frame would allow, he focused on the mission, knowing that any distraction now could get him killed in an instant, and waited to see if the unicorn lookalikes did anything he could use against them.

Having hopped over the side of the ridge, Orac and Keesha headed directly toward the dragon encampment, their mental shields raised, once again thanks to the mantra, both of them knowing not to lower them under any circumstances. They did both however, know the plan, having gone over it in as much detail as they could the previous evening. And so the golden, yellow and orange dragon slowed abruptly before reaching the valley floor, stopping amongst a sea of boulders. Orac dropped down beside her, giving her a conspiratorial wink as he did so. In unison, they picked up the heaviest rocks that they could, and as one, bounded into the fresh air, all the time heading for the sleeping encampment of dragons.

Atop the rocky crest, cloaked in the long drawn out dawn shadows, For'son, his mind protected by Orac's mantra, spotted the slightest movement below, and much like any hunter stalking its prey, waited to see what would happen.

Shaking its head in an effort to become fully awake, unfurling its long tangled mane as it did so, the light brown coloured ra-hoon clambered to its feet, and as silently as possible, not wanting to wake up his cohorts, trotted off in the direction of the light orange stone island that the king's friend and mighty warrior lay atop, much to his astonishment.

'What the...?' thought For'son, until he realised that the unicorn lookalike was doing what most beings do on waking up... going to relieve himself. And in that lay his chance to take out the first of them. Knowing that he needed to be not only quick, but silent as well, in a streak of burnished blue he dropped talons first towards his target.

Wondering what the day would hold, still trying to shake off some of the sleepiness he felt, it was only when a rush of cold air washed over him that he realised something was wrong. But by then... it was too late!

Unusually for any dragon, given their prehistoric, primal desires, For'son, despite his role as the king's primary protector and guardian, had a dislike for any unnecessary violence. Of course he could fight, with him being one of the most courageous, able and decorated of his kind, his valiant deeds and selfless acts renowned across the kingdom, but he didn't act on either a whim or a wont. He fought only when absolutely essential, and even then it went against everything he believed in.

Here and now though, he was in the zone, knowing that not only were Keesha and Orac depending on him, but the rest of the dragons caught in the dreaded mental grip of the ra-hoon's magic. And so he did what he was best at, slicing the singular beast's head from his body in one fell swoop, executing his attack to perfection, even catching most of the monster's mass before it could hit the ground and alert his comrades.

'One down, six to go...' he thought as he kicked sand across the blood he could see, before he picked up both the separated head and the body of the cadaver and with two flaps of his wings, landed back in his previous position, setting the carcass down behind him, knowing there was no way in hell his comrades would find it up there. If he could keep the element of surprise, and sow the seeds of doubt in their minds, that might help his cause a great deal.

Pleased at having taken down one of them, wondering how long it would be before they noticed, out of nowhere something tickled his brain. Instantly alert for any kind of attack, the shield around his mind very much reining in his magical senses, at least for now, what he felt was like a singular rap on a door. And he knew what that meant. His friends were only thirty seconds out from surprising those dragons that were now serving the ra-hoon. And that meant if he wanted to inflict the most chaos and mayhem possible, he had to act... NOW! Shaking his huge primeval head, wondering what the hell he was doing here in the first place, he took one last long deep breath, and stretching out his wings, bounded up into the air in the direction of the unicorn lookalikes, hoping to catch them unawares at exactly the same time his friends stirred up a hornet's nest with the dragons under their control.

Approaching the multitude of sleeping dragons, some she recognised as either friends or kin, about one hundred metres in the air, flying low because what they needed was accuracy rather than anything else, momentarily she looked back into the ever increasing sunlight to make sure the shy and retiring librarian was there right behind her... he was. With that confirmed, and the rocks she'd picked up firmly in the grasp of her talons down below her body, Keesha wished herself luck, checked that the mental barricades around her mind were still intact, and readied herself to act, desperate not to injure any of those below too badly.

Afraid yet full of utter wonder and joy, Orac tailed the most stunning dragon he'd ever actually met by only a few metres, all the time aware of the encampment of dragons below them, something they were approaching rapidly. Thigh muscles burning from the intensity of carrying the two huge rocks beneath his squat little frame, compared with most of his kind, he hoped that he'd hold out until they reached the point at which they could release them. The idea, his in fact, had been to draw the dragons out by making them mad, something he hoped the rocks falling upon them would do, and get them to pursue, the expectation being that it would leave the ra-hoon defenceless and at the mercy of For'son's particular set of skills. About to reach the drop zone, all the introverted librarian could think was... 'GERONIMO!'

Gearing up for his attack, the royal protector brought forth in his mind the words he would need to decimate the ra-hoon, and heading straight for them at speed, prepared to strike. What with, I hear you ask? Lightning, that if used correctly should annihilate each of the rocks that the monsters were sheltering amongst, turning them into the most vicious and effective shrapnel possible, ideally killing and wounding many of them, setting him on his way to what he was sure would become a lethal game of cat and mouse.

Eyes wide open, ready to direct the supernatural power at his disposal, he positively yelled the words inside his head, adding a huge dollop of magic as well as a considerable amount of his willpower. Closing in at speed, arcing bolts of brilliant, fluorescent green lightning splayed out in front of him from his fingertips, not aimed at the creatures themselves due to their immunity, but at the rocks they'd taken shelter amongst, that now, almost as one, splintered and fractured apart as they exploded en masse, causing the earth to quake and the air to scream.

Not a million miles away, at precisely the same time, Keesha reached the point of no return, and praying that they wouldn't harm the dragons below beyond repair and that they could somehow be brought out from under the control of those blessed unicorn lookalikes, dropped the two giant rocks that she'd been holding in both of her feet, before banking around and heading north with as much speed as she could muster. Orac, (very much within DRS range... it's a Formula 1 joke) a split second behind her, followed her lead and let go of his payload, again banking round, flapping his wings as hard as he could in a concerted effort to keep up.

BOOM!

Landing amongst the throng of sleeping dragons, the four rocks and their splintering fragments did untold damage, ripping wings, severing legs, breaking arms and ankles, busting heads as well causing fear and anxiety on an industrial level. Under normal circumstances, dragons being attacked would be formidable opponents, even coming straight out of a deep sleep, but don't forget these had another obstacle to overcome... the fact that they were being controlled by the ra-hoon, their minds not their own, and so they were pitifully slow to respond to what had happened. In fact, it took them nearly a full minute to determine exactly what had gone on, and that they should give chase, something that only about half of them were able to do, which had indeed increased the odds of survival for the three courageous heroes out to stop the ra-hoon from harming any other beings.

Spectacular would be an accurate way to describe the detonation, or correctly, detonations that had resulted from For'son's fluorescent green, magical lightning strikes on the rocks, sending razor sharp superheated stone in every direction, acting as an improvised explosive device would in our modern world, sending tens of thousands of tiny fragments every which way. Not particularly subtle or clinical, it was at least as effective as anything could be, maiming three of their kind there and then, wounding at least two others badly, the last of which remained unharmed through sheer luck and absolutely nothing else. About to move in and rake one of the injured ra-hoon with his talons in an attempt to finish him off, suddenly a piercing wail, followed by the utmost pressure imaginable encompassed his mind, forcing him to veer off course, almost crashing him into the ground... ALMOST! But not quite. For'son was able to sweep around in a tight loop, his gigantic prehistoric frame almost on autopilot, his outstretched talons clipping the ground, but nothing more than that, after which he took to the sky, his wings flapping as hard as they ever had in a desperate attempt to get away and shake off the crushing pressure on his psyche.

Heading in the opposite direction full of anger, rage and venom, the three dozen or so dragons to survive the rock dropping attack unscathed were now in full pursuit of Orac and Keesha, their wings flapping ten to the dozen, each and every one of them expending far more energy than was either healthy or wise, their clouded minds still under the influence of the unicorn lookalikes, despite their masters themselves having more pressing issues to deal with.

"They're gaining on us. I don't think we're going to be outrunning them anytime soon," screamed the stunning golden female over the howling breeze they found themselves flying into.

Against his better judgement, Orac looked over his shoulder. Clapping eyes on all those dragons sent a chill racing from his head down to his tail, one that he could well have done without.

'Talk about seeing the whites of their eyes,' he mused, noting that not a single one of them had an iris showing, something he knew meant they were still being controlled. So much for the theory that they might well have been out of range this far out... if only.

'There's so many of them,' was his next panicked thought, quickly followed by, 'and they've made up quite some ground. What the hell are we going to do?' Just as that popped into his head, half a dozen stray fireballs from the pursuing mob lit up the air all around them as they streaked harmlessly past, a warning if ever there was one about just how much danger they were in.

Against the background noise of the onrushing air, Keesha yelled,

"Follow me," before dropping like a stone and vectoring in on a huge, dark fissure in the ground up ahead.

Without having time to even think about what he was doing, just as another flaming orange and red fireball zipped past his right shoulder, only the heat alerting him to its presence, and terrified beyond belief, the librarian gave himself over to the tug of gravity and, spiralling as he did so, dropped right onto her tail, the G forces involved making his chin and cheeks rattle. It wasn't graceful, it wasn't something to be proud of, but it was necessary if he wanted to stay alive. And he very much did.

The caves were all she could think of, the ones where she'd played and explored as a dragonling, all those decades ago.

'If we can make it to the entrance, they'll only be able to follow us one by one because the narrow passageways make it impossible to do anything else, and my expert recall will give us a huge advantage. Come on, come on,' she urged herself, heading towards the ground like an out of control fighter jet, way too fast and ungainly. Nothing about that mattered though, only getting through the entrance.

While Keesha and Orac headed for the surface at speed, almost the direct opposite could be said of the third of the trio, For'son, who was now powering his way skywards, straight up, determined to put as much distance between him and what remained of the ra-hoon contingent. With the snaking, all consuming pressure attempting to pierce the defences of his mind, it was all that he could do, his flying ungainly and uneconomic, something that everybody that knew him would attest was very much out of character.

Sun rays reflecting off the sweat pouring across all the different shades of his brilliant blue scales, despite the chilling effect of the wind and the upper atmosphere, still his brain felt like a nut in the unyielding grip of a nutcracker, muddling his thoughts, all of his magic diverted, reinforcing that which protected not only his intelligence, but what felt like his soul as well. He could almost feel the deadly, devious minds behind the onslaught, the occasional thought and the sound of horrid laughter barely audible in the background. They wanted to break him, control him, harm him... all of this came across as more of a feeling than one specific thought. Powering on with his mighty wings, one flap at a time, he licked his parched lips in an attempt to take his focus away from the burning muscles and the vicious mental assault. And then it happened, after what must have been nine or ten miles of flying directly up, not quite reaching the troposphere. In a gradual wave of relief, the heaviness haranguing his mind began to subside. Thirty seconds later For'son hovered to a halt, sure by now that he was out of reach of the dastardly unicorn lookalikes, grateful to have survived and inflicted such devastation on their number, but by now, well aware of the threat the beasts posed not only to him, but others of his kind.

'They must be destroyed,' he thought, catching an updraft, gliding along on its warm current, letting it tickle the scales on his belly, his mental defences still very much up, despite the threat seeming to be over, for now at least. Taking stock, allowing his magical reserves to recover just a little, not so much from the new lightning mantra that he'd used, the one procured from the land only just brought under their banner from his last adventure with the king, more so from holding the barriers around his mind in place for such a long period of time, he counted himself lucky to have survived and wondered how his two comrades were faring against the dragon puppets they'd been tasked to distract.

Pulling an almost complete one eighty, Keesha, talons first, hit the peach coloured rock plinth hard, sending snippets of stone flying in all directions, her muscular thighs and knees taking the brunt of the impact. Knowing that her companion was hot on her tail, she leapt down and with as much speed as she could, scrambled sideways through a dark gap between two massive boulders that appeared to be part of the cliff face itself.

Skidding precariously off the plinth that his friend, yes that's how he now thought of her... friend, had landed on only a moment or so before, his body never having ached before as much as it did now, Orac bounded down onto the sandy path and followed it up to the gigantic stones and into the dark in between them both.

"Hurry," urged Keesha, knowing that the mob of murderous dragons were still hot on their tail, the white's of their eyes still showing, much to her disappointment, understanding that they were still under the influence of the despicable unicorn lookalikes.

"I'm right behind you, I'm right behind you," babbled Orac, scared out of his wits, not knowing where they were or what they were doing.

Almost as if sensing this, the stunning golden female tried to tell him her plan whilst they were on the move.

"After the next cavern, the passageway narrows down considerably, with only one of us being able to fit through at a time. That'll slow them down, and maybe give us a chance to get the drop on them."

"Where's the exit come out?" asked the librarian, eager to understand just what they'd got themselves into and whether or not some of their murderous pursuers would be waiting for them on the other side.

Silence... not of the stone cold variety, because they were both moving as fast as they could, kicking up sand and pebbles, brushing against the rock walls on either side of them, more the... awkward kind, something the guardian of all things written picked up on immediately.

"Uhh... there is another way out, isn't there?"

"Umm... not really, no."

"WHAT!" exclaimed Orac. "No way out, what on earth were you thinking?"

"I just thought it would buy us some time, and that maybe they'd give up and return to their masters."

"I can't believe for one second that'll be the case," panted the librarian, suddenly feeling a huge burst of heat from behind him, before being thrown forward at a tremendous rate as the rock wall they stood against exploded into a thousand pieces, peppering them both with stony shrapnel.

Rising to his knees, Keesha pulled him to his feet as the resounding blast echoed around the underground cave system they'd been drawn into, dust and sand filling the air, making it all but impossible to see more than a few metres ahead.

"Come on, quick, we need to make it through the next cavern to the passageway on the far side," insisted the young female.

Knowing that it was less than ideal, but with little alternative, Orac started off after her, concentrating on putting one giant foot in front of the other, as that was about all that he could manage, his ears still ringing, the scales on his right shoulder damaged and burnt, something that really shouldn't have been possible.

Out in the open blue sky, a short way away, For'son's mana had almost fully regenerated, meaning he was all but good to go. But what to do next, that was the question he asked himself. Having gotten a taste of just how powerful the ra-hoon were, he wasn't keen to take them on again. Just having his mind squeezed like that was painful beyond belief. But he knew that for the sake of all the beings in this part of the world, he had to do just that, if he wanted to not only return to his friend the king, but sleep well in the future. Not knowing what else to do, he circled around, caught yet one more updraft in his favour and headed back towards the start of the valley, all the time wondering what he could conjure up that would physically harm the rampant ra-hoon.

Now out in the open deep inside a gargantuan cavern, Keesha and Orac, still some way ahead of their pursuers, dodged fireball after fireball as they sprinted for all they were worth towards the path at the far end, the one that should narrow considerably and at least buy them some time.

Following the waggling golden tail in front of him,

weaving this way and that, trying not to be hit by any of the enemy's fearsome fiery ferociousness, in the midst of it all the librarian suddenly realised that the subterranean grotto they found themselves in was full of crystals, growing out of the rock in almost every direction, in a myriad of different colours, sizes and shapes.

'Fascinating,' he thought, all the time on the move, his wings tucked in by his sides, talons scrabbling for grip on the soft, sandy path. If only he'd had more time, he'd definitely have stopped to investigate the awesome looking gemstones further.

Abruptly an almighty BOOM resonated around the underground space they found themselves trapped in, quickly followed by two more and the sound of crashing rock and stone. These dragons controlled by the will of the unicorn lookalikes had taken to targeting the ceiling above the entrance to the tucked away footpath that they were heading for, clearly hoping to bring enough material down to stop them from escaping. Dangerous couldn't do justice to what they were doing, because they could very easily collapse the entire construct.

Gasping for breath, legs burning with fatigue, Keesha, about to pass the threshold of the narrow footpath, was suddenly sent flying forward by a deadly trio of fireballs from some way back hammering the ceiling directly above, sending tons of debris down in a cloud of dust and devastation. Quickly getting to her feet, she grabbed Orac's hand and pulled him into the narrow passageway, just as the wreckage from up above smashed into the floor, filling most of the entrance.

"That should keep them busy for a while," stated the beautiful golden dragon.

Orac was too busy choking on the dust and remnants to reply, but nodded his understanding as they padded off, hoping to put some distance between them and those chasing.

Reaching the beginning of the valley, aware that he

would be well out of range of the ra-hoon's deadly mental abilities, For'son touched down on the warm yellow sand, his bright blue feet relishing the feeling as his mind wondered what he should do next. He was sure that there were only three of the monstrous beasts left, but given what they could do, even one would have been a challenge like no other. And the fact that they couldn't be touched by anything supernatural presented a real problem. Of course he'd already gotten around that by exploding the rock with the fabulous lightning mantra that he'd picked up from the tiny dank library on his last mission, but that wouldn't work a second time. Briefly, he wondered what would.

Thankfully, at least for the librarian, they'd slowed down to a walk, sure that, for the time being, they weren't being followed.

Having switched over to her infrared vision some time ago, Keesha led the way, memories of the crystal lined walkways from her youth filling her mind, games of chase and hide and seek with her friends and family, those that were even at this moment hunting them down with a view to doing goodness knows what, tainting everything. Pushing all that aside upon reaching a slightly wider part of the passage, the golden, yellow and orange coloured female stopped to see if her companion was alright.

"How are you holding up?" she asked.

"Okay... I suppose. I have to say though I didn't expect to be trapped underground facing a mad horde of ra-hoon influenced dragons. Are you sure there's no other way out?"

"I haven't been down here for a couple of decades, but I'm absolutely certain there's nothing, no other exit. In about a kilometre, the path opens out into one single cave full of crystals which is just a dead end. That's it, all that I have. I'm sorry if I've made a mistake in bringing us down here," she said, her lips wobbling just slightly, the repository guardian picking up on her momentary distress.

"It wasn't a criticism, youngster, far from it in fact. I don't doubt for a moment that had we stayed out in the open, we would, by now at least, be surrounded and captured, or probably worse. I'd much rather be in here and alive, thank you very much."

That did at least seem to do the trick, a slight smile creeping over the golden female's face.

"Come on, let's get down to the cavern at the end, you'll be blown away when you see it."

And with that, the two strolled off in the direction of the dead end that might well prove to be their last stand, all the time listening out for any sign of pursuit.

Reinforcing the mantra that should protect his mind, feeling it enclose his intelligence immediately, For'son, having already stretched out with his magical senses to try and find his friends, without any luck, wished them well with whatever it was they were facing, unwilling to even consider that something bad had happened to them. Knowing that he could put a stop to all of it by once and for all defeating the unicorn lookalikes, he readied his magic, took one huge breath, and with the focus and determination of a true warrior, bounded into the air in the direction of the beasts that were his primary target.

Cutting through the humid morning breeze about three metres off the ground, the king's friend and prodigious warrior selected what he regarded as the right mantra for the job, whispered the words in his mind, all the time applying his considerable will and no small amount of magic. Suddenly in his wake, all hell broke loose as sand, boulders and stones leapt into the air behind him, all seemingly of their own accord, swirling, whirling and twirling around, almost as if he'd snagged the mother of all hurricanes, towing it in his wake.

Twelve or so miles away, three very angry, upset and injured (well... two of them anyway) ra-hoon stood over the cadavers of their kind, understandably distraught at what had happened. Their leader, a being that went by the name of Stuffi, the only one to come out of For'son's unexpected attack unharmed, knew that now was not the time for mourning, not with the dragon responsible for all this still out there somewhere, protected to some degree by unfamiliar magic. And as he'd attacked once, Stuffi knew there was a good chance he would come back and try to finish the job. And so against his instincts, he rallied the other two, startling them out of their grief, reminding them of their responsibilities and triggering their inborn need for revenge. Should their unidentified aggressor return they'd be ready and waiting, the full might of their combined strength on standby, knowing that nothing and no one in the past had ever resisted that.

Three minutes, that's how long it took them to reach the cavern at the end of the little used path, and although deeply unhappy at being trapped, there was at least a bright side for the librarian dragon, something he commented on immediately.

"Wow!"

"Oh yeah... I forgot to mention how it might appear to an outsider."

"It's amazing," gushed Orac, absolutely entranced by not only the colours and depths of the crystals in the cave, but by their sheer number and size. By his count alone, and he was a wizard when it came to maths, there must easily have been over a million, maybe even two, growing out of every surface, even on occasion sprouting up from the ground.

"What should we do?" Keesha asked, only now willing to admit to herself that she'd made the wrong call, and by the looks of things, doomed them both.

It was exactly at that point that the repository guardian dropped to his knees, clutching his head with both hands, scrabbling about on the sandy floor, evidently in a serious amount of pain.

"Orac, Orac, what is it, what's happening?"

If he could have focused, he would have done so, but

the sheer volume of noise, words and different memories had him not only bamboozled but in absolute agony. All he'd done was open up the most minute gap in the defensive shield around his mind in an effort to see if could get a message out to his friend, the king's protector. Nothing should have been able to get through, he was sure of that, but on doing so, out of nowhere, there was all of this. You'd think he could just plug the hole, extend his barrier out so that no gap appeared, both of which he did, but it didn't seem to matter now. Dozens of voices, all seeming rather benign and robotic, almost as if they didn't have minds of their own, bombarded his intellect, the combination of them all overwhelming, all consuming, terrifying him to his very core. Hunched over on the floor, digging around in the sand, about to give up, his thoughts suddenly turned to For'son, the dragon he now regarded as his friend, and as they did so, two things happened.

One, instantly his confidence grew, whether from the admiration for his pal, or just knowing that he'd do more, somehow prevail against all odds, and that allowed him to start to separate all the different noises and individuals he could feel within his psyche.

And two, unbelievably given the distance separating them, he could actually feel the dragon himself, having just taken flight, at the entrance to the valley if he wasn't mistaken, and he was sure that he wasn't, on some last death dealing run, determined to take down the ra-hoon once and for all. It was amazing, astounding and totally impossible. That is until he picked his huge prehistoric head up off the floor and noticed for the first time that the crystals around him seemed to be glowing.

'What the...?' he thought, astounded at what was going on, until a soft voice interrupted the flow of his thoughts.

"Orac... are you okay? What's happening?"

Composing himself, his confidence returned in no small part due to For'son, he stood up and as he did so, the crystals higher up on the walls surrounding them started to light up.

"Uh... what's going on?" asked Keesha again, concerned for her friend.

"I... I... I'm not sure. Suddenly I was overwhelmed by... not so much voices, but thoughts invading the space in my head. I think it might be the dragons under the control of the ra-hoon."

"The ones chasing us?"

"Yes."

"What does that mean? Have they somehow developed the same powers as their masters?"

"No... I don't think it's that. I do however believe that whatever's happening is somehow related to these crystals," the librarian added, running one of his hands along the gemstones on one wall.

"Why do you think that?"

"Because they didn't attack me, and I could sense For'son some way off in the distance."

"Is he okay?"

"I think he is, but I believe he's about to do something reckless, and could well need our help."

"That's impossible, trapped inside here as we are."

"Yes," replied Orac, his brain working overtime as to exactly what he'd stumbled on to. "When you were here all those decades ago, did anything... weird happen?"

"Define weird."

"I don't know... anything at all unusual, out of the ordinary."

"I don't think so. No, hang on, wait. On the odd occasion when we were playing hide and seek throughout all the chambers, I was able to... almost sense where my friends were concealed, and I was always right when that happened, almost as if I could feel where their minds were, despite however closed down or faraway they were."

"Excellent!"

"I think I know what these crystals do."

"And what's that?"

"At a guess, and it's only that, I believe the crystals somehow boost or enhance our telepathic powers, extending the range by quite some distance."

"Is that even a thing?"

"It is now."

"Can we get a message to For'son to make him stop what he has in mind?"

"I've tried, and although I can sense his presence, I can't break down the barriers he has around his intellect to defend against the ra-hoon."

"Oh," sighed Keesha. "What do we do now?"

Right at that moment, a loud crashing echoed down the subterranean corridor towards their position. Clearly their pursuers had fought their way past the debris and were heading towards their position.

"I have an idea," announced Orac, "but I'm not sure if it'll work."

"Whatever it is, we'd better do it quickly."

"If my hypothesis is correct, then the crystals surrounding us should amplify our telepathic abilities tenfold. If we both stand in different parts of it, we can attempt to use the gemstones."

"To do what?"

"I can try and appeal to the good in them in the hope that something in their original personalities remembers. And you can flood them with all of your memories, whether childhood or recent. Get them to recall. If that happens, maybe they can break through whatever the ra-hoon are using to coerce them."

"Understood," replied the young female.

"I'll stay at the front," suggested Orac, trying to be both brave and chivalrous. "You take up a position at the back."

"When do we start?"

"Straight away... the crystals should allow us to bombard their minds easily over this distance."

Sprinting to the back of the cavern, running her tiny

hands across the top of the intriguing, beautiful purple, white, blue, green, red and yellow crystals surrounding her, Keesha nodded to the librarian, signalling that she was ready.

Scared beyond belief, his legs wobbling like a jelly riding a bike down a cobbled hill, Orac closed his eyes, swallowed nervously, attempted to find his focus, and reached out using all of his supernatural power in an effort to find those that would do them harm.

Standing out like a vegan at a butcher's, the dragon presences were easy to pinpoint, although they did feel a little strange. Normally you would expect their essences to be a bright beacon of light, shining through their surroundings, but although these were obviously dragons heading towards them, they appeared subdued, dull and dampened down, clearly the control the unicorn lookalikes had over them rearing its ugly head. No matter.

Barely breathing, which is not a problem for any of their kind, the dedicated librarian sought out the individual entities that he could feel and with the crystals all around him lit up like a Christmas tree, he bombarded them with as much goodwill as he could, using feelings and words that depicted friendship, family, community, teamwork, spirit and everything else righteous he could think of. It was a long shot, but since they were trapped with nowhere else to go it was the only thing available. He was also quite optimistic that it would work, given the amazing powers of the gemstones surrounding them.

Keesha, aware of the trouble heading their way and more than a little afraid, tucked all of that to one side and extended her mind out in the direction of the passageway and the oncoming horde, albeit one by one, of dragons that she knew. Given the substantial difference between their fundamental natures normally and now, how they were under the influence of the ra-hoon, it was difficult, but if she concentrated hard, briefly she could just determine the individuals beneath the blanket of restraint and repression. And so she focused on them to start with, sharing memories of happier times, get-togethers, community events and activities, as well as more personal, one on one encounters. With the crystals bolstering her abilities, it was easier to share all of this with the multitude of beings heading their way, simultaneously showering them all with the love and care that she felt for each of them and their previous way of life. Whether or not it was having an effect was anyone's guess.

Further back in the underground tunnels, the ra-hoon's minions, all in single file, stomped ever forward, having cleared the debris that had blocked their way for so long, like the zombified soldiers that they were, one goal driving them forward: to find their attackers and kill them. Somewhere in the back of what remained of their intellect was the notion that this was a dead end and that they were trapped, sparking off a tiny sliver of delight inside their robot-like minds. About half a kilometre away now, they all knew as one collective that there was no escaping for their prey.

Dragging what looked very much like a hurricane in his wake, For'son, fearsome warrior and king's protector, sped down the valley, the vicious swirling mass behind him picking up everything, rocks, stones, plants, animals and insects, all the time his mind walled off as he closed in on the ra-hoon's last known position, determined to rain down hell on the unicorn lookalikes and end their dominance.

What he didn't know though, was that the devious and cunning contingent still left alive, knew that he was coming. Not because they could break down his defences and feel his mind, for once not being able to penetrate the supernatural spell that kept his mental faculties safe. No, they could feel the walled off magic of the mantra itself and were able to track it from quite some distance. And so with that in mind Stuffi, their leader, ordered the other two to take up positions either side of him on the valley floor and face the dragon who'd torn their grouping apart and killed their kin. There would be a reckoning for what had gone on previously, and that particular dragon would pay the price for his insolence.

Knowing that things might get hairy fast, the beating heart of the warrior inside the king's friend readied itself for action, reflexes on alert, battle hardened experience primed to be of use, offensive mantras only a fraction of a second from being applied. For all intents and purposes, For'son was as prepared as he could be to take down one hell of an almighty foe, one that he didn't understand and that magic couldn't supposedly harm. For him, it would be an adventure into the unknown. Whether he'd savour the taste of victory, only time would tell.

Spread out across the valley, with Stuffi in the middle, the two injured ra-hoon either side of him, still desperately trying to heal their wounds with borrowed dragon magic that they couldn't quite make work as effectively as the winged prehistoric beasts themselves, not only could they get an impression of their prey now through their magically enhanced senses, they could also hear the tempestuous twister destroying anything in its path that accompanied the dragon on his onrushing assault. Fear was something that none of them had ever experienced before, but one of their kind, now hobbling intently because of a broken leg damaged in the attack and a fractured jaw, stood on the left side of the valley, very much rethinking her life choices. Here and now, the whole debacle of taking over the dragon villages, which had seemed like a cunning and potentially life changing plot at the time, now appeared to be coming back to bite them on the ass, big time. There were much easier prey and food sources out there she knew, something that if she could go back, would make her hesitate to be involved in the course of action that they'd taken. And so continuing with the below par healing, pain and fear coursing through her, one particular piece of magic that she'd picked up from a species of serpent that they'd coerced many, many years ago, sprang to the front of her intellect, presenting her with an opportunity, should she wish, to escape at a moment's notice. In her mind, she hoped it wouldn't come to that.

Back in the subterranean tunnel and cave system that Orac and Keesha found themselves trapped in, the two buddies and brave dragons were only moments away from their enemies, the friends and kin of the golden female, from the surrounding villages, almost on top of them.

Exhaling, Orac turned to his companion on this fantastical adventure and urged her on, telling her that they both needed to double their efforts. Taking his words on board, she did just that, recalling everything that was special to her from the villages she'd grown up in, not now concentrating on any one individual, but sending all of the images, words and sounds out in the direction of all the mind controlled dragons that were heading their way.

Briefly, about halfway down the dark stony passage, the all white eyes of a squat green and brown female changed for but a split second, the irises returning, her mind rid of the shadowy mist that kept her from thinking and her personality at bay. But that's as good as it got, with the rahoon's will soon overriding any other compunctions, snuffing out the bright light and the faintest of hope.

It had worked, just for a second... he could feel it, off in the distance. One of them had come back. Delight rippled through him at the thought that they were on the right track and that it could actually be done. All they needed now was to pull it off on all of them at the same time, which given the leaders were now only seconds away from being upon them, would be quite something. No pressure then!

"It's working," he shouted turning back towards Keesha. "But we need more. Give it everything you have. It's now all or nothing!"

Magic coursing through their primeval bodies in one

last blazing telepathic, not so much attack or assault, as display of the previous lives they'd had, the librarian and the exquisite gold dragon gave everything over to the task in front of them, knowing that if they failed they were as good as dead, also aware that they held the last chance for the villagers, some of whom were her family. With only a few seconds to play out, the mischievous entity known as Fate watched on from afar with a glint in her eye, hoping at the very least to be entertained. She wouldn't be disappointed.

Extravagantly barrel rolling now, rotating axially at speed in front of the gigantic beast of the stormy hurricane that he towed in his wake, he could just about see all three of the monstrous fiends spread out in front of him on the valley floor, each looking stoic and defiant, almost as if they didn't have a care in the world, something he found hard to believe.

'It's an act,' he thought, knowing that there was little they could do to either stop him or what lay behind him, from hitting them like a ton of bricks. They would, he knew, die a perilous and painful death. And then, about four hundred metres out... it happened! Belched from each of their mouths, a constant stream of mesmerising yellow, orange, red and blue fireballs closed in on his position.

'That's... impossible,' was the only thought he could conjure up as he not only spun, but rocketed forwards at about half the speed of sound, the whistling wind and debris behind him by now, casting a huge shadow where the sun should have been. Immediately his quick and experienced battle hardened brain kicked in, trying to provide him with a solution. Unfortunately, it had never seen anything like this, wondering how on earth each of them could produce an array of fireballs in a row like that, because dragons certainly couldn't. But there was no time to waste thinking. All that mattered now was how to avoid the fiery death crisscrossing his path in all but a moment or two. His life very much depended on how he dealt with this, he knew.

Disappointingly, they'd reached the point of no return and hadn't succeeded in bringing the dragons that were all but upon them out of their trance-like states.

Rushing in with only murderous intent on their minds, one, two, three, four, five... half a dozen dragons, accompanied by blood curdling screams, propelled themselves forward, some sprinting, others giving a little flap of their wings, only able to bound at speed as opposed to actually flying because of the confined space, all converging on Orac's position as he was the closest to them. Aware of what was going on, the courageous and dedicated librarian stood as still as a statue, eyes closed, still using his telepathy to inundate his attackers with thoughts of peace and goodwill, knowing now that this was, for him at least, the end. Twenty metres away, Keesha did the same, flooding the newcomers with all her warm and caring thoughts, putting every last ounce of passion and willpower behind her magic, desperately hoping it would be enough. But would it?

With events spiralling out of control at jet fighter speed, For'son's adaptable, intelligent and crafty mind could only come up with one solution. It was far from ideal: avoiding action. That, he knew, meant any number of risks, for him at least. Dropping right down to the surface of the valley floor, feeling the sand tickle his underbelly, he swished his huge blue shaded tail and wheeled off to one side, hoping for two things. One... that he could successfully avoid the worst of the windswept hell that was coming in at high speed behind him, and two... that the crazy, all out tornado-like mass filled with sand, stone, rubble, trees and animals would carry on and assault the creatures it was meant to take down. As the fireballs intended to take him down zipped over his head, gobbled up by the ferocity behind him, his wishes disappeared and reality caught up with him.

Pouring on as much speed as his wings would allow at

this height, he swooped across in front of the storm he'd been towing, readjusting his trajectory, aiming for the rocky side of the valley, hoping to clear the deadliness that his magic had created. Two seconds in, hope died as the freezing cold air, debris and fragments of goodness knows what hit him like a sledgehammer pummelling a weak wall. In that moment, he was wolfed down by the chaos, caught up in its misery and power, tumbling about in the shadows like a handkerchief in a hurricane. Unable to fly, think or even breathe, the brave and fearsome warrior's fate depended on the elements of his own making.

One piece of fortune though, was that his second hope came true... the grey and black, shadowy monstrosity continued on its way, momentum forcing it forward despite losing the tip of its spear. Without warning, and much to their surprise, the ra-hoon were taken, flung up into the air, their unicorn shaped bodies tossed around and around in a funnel of high velocity wind, pummelling and pounding, relentless in its ferocity, taking away what magic was available to them, causing them all, for once, to be afraid for their lives.

A split second away from striking, the two gargantuan dragons that must have only just fitted through the passageway itself, towered over the shy and timid librarian, about to pummel him to dust. Jaws open, teeth bared, fierce and brutal snarls engrained across the scales of their prehistoric faces, about to annihilate one of their own, suddenly the whites of their eyes reversed completely, returning to what they would have once regarded as normal. As more of their kind skidded to a halt in the cool, yellow sand, confusion reigned with the masses unable to comprehend either where they were, or why they were here.

Through a combination of Orac and Keesha boosting their telepathic powers by using the rainbow array of crystals in the cave, and the ra-hoon getting sucked up into the vicious vortex of high winds and death defying darkness, the abominations that were the unicorn lookalikes had lost, at least for now, their grip on the dragon villagers, in the kind of timing that only Lady Luck could have come up with. Fate looked on, intrigued to see what would happen next.

"I... I... I don't understand," the garbled words spat out of the first of the dinosaur-like monsters to race into the cavern, the one currently hovering directly over Orac.

Before the stunned librarian could say a word, Keesha, from further back amongst the crystals, came forward.

"It's okay G'rth... he's a friend. Stand down!"

As confused as ever, the gentle giant of a dragon did as the young female he'd known since birth commanded, now aware of others pouring into the subterranean grotto.

"What... what... what are we all doing here?" echoed a familiar voice, at least to Keesha anyway, one that she was most grateful to hear, even more than the rest, not because she hoped that they would come to harm, far from it in fact given her heroics across the day. No, because this was her... MOTHER!

"MOTHER," she yelled, barrelling forward, barging others out of the way, throwing herself into the pink and purple hued dragon's arms without any other thought in the world.

"I'm so grateful that you're okay," the youngster whispered, despite the fact that every other being there could hear with their enhanced magical senses.

"Why wouldn't I be?" asked her mother inquisitively.

"It's just that..."

"STOP!" shouted the librarian, raising his voice as loud as he could, attracting everyone's attention. "We don't have time for this. If you're all to remain safe, you must all learn this mantra and enact it straight away."

"Of course," mumbled Keesha, cursing herself for not realising immediately that the others were still very much at risk of being overwhelmed by the ra-hoon. "Do as he says," she yelled. "He's a friend from a faraway land and has managed to save you all from a particularly unedifying fate."

This got them all gossiping.

"Enough!" growled the young golden, yellow and orange dragon, putting some venom behind her words this time in an effort to convey just how serious she was, something that caused all of them to be quiet. "Orac here is going to recite to you the words of a mantra. You will immediately apply them in your mind with as much willpower and magic as you can. This should keep you safe, at least for the time being, from those damn unicorn lookalikes. Do it now!"

And so the repository guardian did, with as much haste as he could, careful to get it right. Once finished, to a dragon, all of the villagers applied it to themselves, something that immediately became evident.

"Now would you care to explain exactly what's been going on... little one?" asked Keesha's mother, a graceful looking dragon by the name of Lil'th, who, staring down at her daughter, right here, right now, looked like a dragon not to be messed with.

"You've all been under the influence of the ra-hoon, those dreadful unicorn lookalikes, for days now. You chased the both of us in here. We used our telepathy combined with the crystals in this cave to snap you out of it. The mantra should give you all at least some limited protection from their mental attacks. Keep it up at all times."

"And what about the creatures themselves?" one voice enquired, floating out over the top of all the others there.

"DAMN!" cursed Orac, disappointed with himself for not realising it sooner, knowing that his friend was still out there, in the middle of God knows what.

"What is it?" asked his young companion.

Taking a second or two to reply, because he'd sent part of his mind off in the direction of his comrade in an effort to garner more information, all that he got in return was an inky black kind of chaos. They needed to move, and they needed to move fast.

"For'son," he replied. "He's in trouble... we have to get to him."

"Who the hell is For'son?" implored G'rth, now starting to get a better grip on things going on around him.

Before the librarian had a chance, his stunning companion butted in.

"He's the king's protector, a dragon that's come all this way to save us, and one we no doubt owe a huge debt to. He's in trouble, fighting those monsters further up the valley. Please... we have to go and help him."

With not a decision to be made, and not one single one amongst them hesitating even slightly, the rowdy rabble of villagers, with their intellects now their own, started to storm back up the underground corridor, only one thing on their minds... to save the dragon that had become their salvation.

In the dreadnought of a storm that now enveloped almost a quarter of the valley, the wind had taken on a life of its own, not powered by the supernatural now, but by the dark, vengeful thoughts of those trapped within, and by that I don't mean the brave, light-sided warrior that the king regarded as his best friend. No. I mean those diabolical unicorn lookalikes that thought nothing of others or using violence as a means to an end.

Trapped, using his vast experience to ride the turbulent and buffeting winds all but an impossibility, For'son was tossed around like a rag doll in a washing machine, debris pummelling his ancient scaled body causing him no end of harm, the damaging gusts tugging at his exposed weak spots, tearing holes in his powerful wings, at one point almost ripping off the right one. In absolute agony, magic of no use at all even if he had been able to concentrate enough to use it, all he could do was let nature, or in this case, the ethereal energy that he himself had let loose, take its course.

For the ra-hoon, all three scared out of their mind, it was pretty much the same, each getting tossed around violently, careering into not only all the whirling stone, rocks, plants and wildlife, but each other. They were a hardy race, that's for sure, but even they weren't faring well in the midst of the severe winds and the tempestuous nature of everything going on. Something had to give. And it did.

Abruptly the magic, or rather the propensity for evil died, instantly vanquishing the harsh, angry typhoon that had torn up nearly half the valley. In one last hurrah, everything within was spewed out onto the dust filled and debris ridden chewed up ground, leaving an absolute mess, one in which there were very few survivors. Plants and animals had died in their thousands, as had one of the injured ra-hoon, the body of which lay coated in blood and guts, both its horns shattered, that in itself enough to deal the killer blow. The other, the female whose doubts had almost gotten the better of her earlier, had suffered a few minor injuries, a twisted ankle, a torn hoof, a bleeding cut above her left eye, but nothing that would stop her fighting. However, those doubts had torn her consciousness in two during her brief rollercoaster ride inside what felt like the mother of all hurricanes. And so on finding herself still alive and pretty much in one piece, she stumbled to her feet, selected the words that she'd stolen from another's mind quite some time ago, and applying a little of the ransacked dragon magic that still remained inside her, in one fell swoop, became totally and utterly invisible. Not wanting anything more to do with the struggle that was going on in the valley against the dragon villagers, figuring that even from the start they'd been way out of their depth, slowly she cantered off in a northerly direction, determined to find more of her kind, share the warning of what had happened here, which, given how the ra-hoon's memories can become engrained in their very DNA, could potentially serve their kind for millennia, and live a long and peaceful life. Amongst the chaos, not that anybody would have picked up on it, a set of four hoof prints padded off into the distance, sticking to the flat of the land, avoiding any kind of population.

And that left one, well... one ra-hoon at least. Stuffi, whether through fortune or fortitude had survived with only a few minor cuts and grazes, having used his skill and cunning to erect a rudimentary magical shield, something he'd procured from one of the villagers who'd been experimenting with such a thing. While it hadn't kept him totally safe, it had deflected the worst of it, making him one of the luckiest beings alive. The same could not be said of the courageous, mighty blue warrior that had started all this off some time ago at the head of the valley. Lying deathly still, half buried by a pile of orange rock that had been flung out of the sky, both wings draped across the ground at excruciating angles, the king's friend and protector was out cold, barely breathing, at the mercy of absolutely anything or anyone.

Disorientated and covered in sand and dust, gathering his wits, something of a challenge given exactly what he'd just been through, despite the fact that he was still in one piece, Stuffi scrambled to his feet in an attempt to take in the situation. For as far as he could see, the landscape was wrecked, the cold hard rock cracked and broken, tiny fissures opened up where previously there had been none, sand and dust sparkling throughout the air, and stone and rock tossed asunder. Then, through a haze of debris, a tiny glint of blue caught his attention, and the cold calculating grip of evil that so often drove him on asserted itself with its full force. Shaking off his minor injuries, slowly he trotted over towards what was left of the dragon that had done so much damage, determined to make him pay should there be even the tiniest spark of life left inside him. Reaching the prehistoric winged monster's battered and broken body, on first examination it was clear to him that the beast was still alive, noticing tiny movements of his chest rising and falling. As a delicious smile crept across his horse-like face, he briefly wondered where he should start. Invading his enemy's mind would be child's play, ripping apart his thoughts, memories and will. That was always delightful. Perhaps forcing him to hurt himself, he mused, but maybe not straight away because that, fun as it was, usually made a superb aperitif. And so knowing that the very first thing he had to do was bring him round, Stuffi raised his front leg, and adding all the power he could, stamped his hoof down on the dragon's clearly damaged kneecap in an attempt to get a reaction. Boy did that work.

Instinctively For'son's huge primeval body reacted as only it could, eliciting a ferocious dragon howl that rang out across the valley, snorts and licks of orange and yellow flame roaring out of his mouth and nose simultaneously.

"Welcome back," observed the sadistic unicorn lookalike, pleased at how events had turned around, with him now having the upper hand.

"Uhhhhh..." sighed the broken blue dragon, pain igniting in every single part of his body from the damage it had suffered being thrown around in the middle of the almighty hurricane that he'd deliberately created.

"I suppose you think you're clever, taking down my kind like you did. Let me assure you here and now, you're going to pay one hell of a price for what you've done, of that I can assure you. But before we get down to that," continued the ra-hoon leader, stamping on the shaded blue dragon's broken wing with one of his other hooves, causing an outrageous cry of pain, "I'd like to know just who you are and exactly what you're doing here."

Mind and body on fire, the agony coursing through him, For'son could barely arrange his thoughts, let alone reply to the questions.

"I can take the information that I want from you,

something I'm sure you're well aware of. Your choice!"

The very last thing he wanted was the monstrous beast inside his head, and so the king's friend fought with all that he had, just to reply.

"I... I... I... I was sent by the dragon king," coughed For'son, nearly choking on all the dust and sand he'd swallowed whilst being tossed round and around inside the hurricane he'd created.

"Why?"

"Because one of the villagers came to us, informing us what you were doing."

"And you're his best response?"

All that For'son could do was cough and nod his head from his trapped position on the floor.

Out of nowhere, Stuffi the ra-hoon leader threw back his pale grey head, his long scraggy mane flailing all over the place and sent skywards a huge roaring laugh, which sounded more menacing than anything else.

With the ra-hoon's attention elsewhere, For'son knew that he had exactly one chance to act and in his mind, he did just that. Unfortunately, nothing happened, because he was simply too broken, in way too much pain. He had no access to his magic, not that a direct attack would have worked, no way to get up and deliver a killing blow, no way to call out telepathically for help, not that he could see how any would arrive, having absolutely no idea where his friends were, or if they were even still alive. In that exact moment, his hope died, and despite not knowing it, he resigned himself to a very painful and undragon-like end.

"Halfway up the valley, somewhere on the left," Orac screamed, as he flew in the midst of a pack of about two dozen dragons, answering the question that had just been asked of him... about the exact whereabouts of his friend.

"On it," was the reply from the leader of the pack, adjusting their trajectory by just a tiny amount.

Only then, with his telepathic senses still stretched out, did the librarian realise the extent of For'son's predicament.

"He's in real trouble. We have to get there NOW!"

Surging forward that bit more, accelerating towards the ground, the scales on their faces contracting just a little due to the forces applied to them, the orange and yellow cloud of sand, stone and debris suddenly started to clear slightly, revealing an all grey horse-like shape hovering over the unmoving broken body of a sparkling, bright, blue shaded dragon. Out of pure reflex, each and every one them found just a touch more speed, and almost acting as one, set aim for the unicorn lookalike protagonist, one all-out head on attack their aim, keen to do everything in their power to save the dragon that had gone some way to freeing them from their enforced servitude.

Still shaken from his rollercoaster ride in the twisting tornado, and distracted by the idea of getting his revenge on the only being that had ever bested him, with his back and tail facing the oncoming dragon horde, he had no sense of what was about to happen. But peeking through the ra-hoon's legs, past its fluffy stomach, the brave, courageous and selfless warrior, unable to move, bereft of his magic, caught sight of what could very well be his salvation. Knowing all he had to do was buy a little more time, For'son fought through the pain and attempted to get the malicious creature's attention.

"Why do you do what you do?" he croaked. "Surely working together with other species would be a better way? Dragons everywhere try their best on a daily basis to improve not only their lives, but the lives of others. They'd gladly share what they have if asked. That's all you have to do."

Reining in the laughter, showing his huge, bright white teeth in a massive sneer, Stuffi had decided to end things there and then, wanting nothing more than to move on to another region, eager to rebuild what he hoped would eventually become some kind of empire. But before he did, he would grant the being before him an answer. He supposed that was the least he could do, something that would turn out to be his total and utter downfall.

"Why ask when it's possible to take? Unlike you, we can plunder exactly what we want, at any moment at all. Not one single being thinks of us as prey, because we're simply too powerful. You might consider your own race to be at the top of the food chain, but I assure you that we, the ra-hoon, are the apex predators across the planet. Nothing can harm us, and there isn't a single being that can resist our mind control."

With that he stood there, the snarl on his face turning into something that could only be described as smug. And that, For'son knew, was only a moment or two from being wiped away forever, as a horde of fast moving dragons closed in on their position.

"Now it's time for you to see firsthand just how pow..."

That was as far as the ra-hoon, the all round apex predator got, before the first three dragons, travelling as fast as they could, took part of him each, the outside ones taking a leg, whilst the one in the middle wrapped his massive prehistoric jaws around his torso, clamping down immediately, the monster's life over in the blink of an eye.

Landing with a THUMP beside their friend, Orac and Keesha both knelt down beside his head, determined to support him in any way possible.

"You're both still alive... fantastic!" were the first words he spoke, unable to see exactly what had happened to the ra-hoon, but assuming that by now it was already dead. And he'd have been right.

"Stay still," urged the beautiful and graceful golden coloured dragon, knowing exactly what was about to happen.

Before Orac had a chance to tell his friend just how pleased he was to see him, a dull white light, starting in the middle of his chest, gradually working its way out to the tips of his wings, started to envelop him.

Briefly, he cried out, not in pain, but more from surprise at what was happening. And what was that, I hear you ask. The rest of the villagers, Keesha's kin and friends, were all healing him with their magic, simultaneously. It was a fantastic spectacle as to what could be achieved by working together and said a great deal about not only their supernatural power, but their knowledge of the dragon physique.

In less than a minute it was done, For'son able to sit up at first, shaking off the rubble and rocks that had landed on him, before eventually rising to his feet, stretching out his powerful, light blue wings, astounded at feeling almost back to full health. Without warning, both his friends enfolded him in one giant hug, their pleasure at seeing him well again not able to be contained any more.

"Thank you," the royal protector ventured in the direction of the crowd, grateful for what they'd done.

"I think it's us that should be thanking you, For'son," replied Lil'th, Keesha's mother. "Without your timely intervention we'd be lost forever, and so undoubtedly, would many more dragons. I hope you'll stay with us for a few days so that we can show you our appreciation and express our gratitude."

Not knowing what else to do, he just nodded in reply, glad that between them all, they'd taken care of the dastardly ra-hoon.

They had, all but one of them who wouldn't be a concern now, but might well come back and haunt him at some point in the future, not that he, or even Fate, would know that, right there and then.

And so the next couple of days were spent healing the rest of the wounded dragons, rebuilding all the settlements, some of which had been devastated by For'son's impromptu hurricane, others by the despicable orders of the unicorn lookalikes that they'd vanquished, as well as making up for the lost food, something put right by the many hunting parties that were sent out. By the second day, things were almost back to normality for the villagers, something that Orac and For'son couldn't have been more pleased about.

"So now do you see how sometimes brain over brawn is a much more effective option?" asked the timid librarian, who'd not only survived his first mission outside the dragon capital, but had actually thrived under extremely challenging circumstances.

"I grant you, what you and Keesha did worked exceedingly well, but what you're forgetting is that without taking the fight to them, the ra-hoon would still be alive, and no doubt intent on revenge or taking back control of all the villagers. But I understand your point, and what you're putting forward. Perhaps we can both agree that the use of intellect and physicality in combination is probably the best way to go and has served us well on this occasion."

Not normally one to climb down from any strong views he held, and this was right up there for him, Orac acknowledged with a singular nod that his pal had a point as they chewed on yet more roasted lamb, something of a change for both of them, as they normally ate it raw.

Against the backdrop of some of the younger dragons amongst the villagers having a fireball contest, attempting to knock down targets over one hundred metres away in an effort to see who could achieve the greatest accuracy, Keesha appeared amidst the two of them, deftly sitting down next to the librarian, much to his delight. A little too much, thought For'son, a smile playing out of the darkest of the blue scales around his face, something that didn't go unnoticed.

"What?" exclaimed the young golden dragon that had been instrumental in their success.

"It's nothing," he answered, not wanting to tease or embarrass the dragon he now thought of as a firm friend, something that before this particular mission he'd never really considered, although now looking back on it, he probably should have.

"Hmm..." mused Keesha.

"What's up?" queried Orac, very much wanting to change the topic of conversation.

"The villagers and I were wondering if you could stay a little longer. It's been such a pleasure having you both around for the last couple of days, and it's not often we get visitors out this far. Everyone agrees that picking your brains about what's going on back in London has made a world of difference to us, knowing that we're not forgotten about and that help is at hand should we ever need it."

"That would give me a chance to study the cave crystals," added Orac, looking hopefully in For'son's direction, as it was he that would have the final say.

"Okay... we'll stay for two more days. But after that," he announced, "it will definitely be time to get back. The king might well need us, particularly if there's any movement on the Ahrensburg situation."

The librarian nodded enthusiastically, while Keesha pumped her fists, happy that both of them could stay a little longer.

Across the next forty eight hours, Orac, Keesha and her mother Lil'th ventured back into the network of subterranean tunnels and caves, both mother and daughter eager to help the librarian understand the rainbow crystals' telepathy boosting properties, both pleased to be reunited with one another.

For'son, in the meantime, got to know all the villagers as best he could, sharing new and unique mantras that he'd picked up on his travels, talking to them in groups about what the king had planned for dragonkind, new and innovative processes, buildings and inventions, as well as assuring them that help would always be there should they need it again. Reassured and almost spellbound by the royal protector's savvy, knowledge and magical knowhow, they took to him like a duck to water, constantly offering him food, drink and their unconditional friendship.

It was much the same for Orac, who despite being possibly the most reserved, shy and timid dragon of all time, had still managed to flourish in an environment as foreign as was possible. And it was clear that the exceptionally beautiful young golden dragon, Keesha, and her mother, had both taken a shine to the selfless librarian. Things were going swimmingly, as was Orac's progress with the crystals in the cave, something he was eager to tell For'son about later that evening.

Chomping down on more roasted lamb, the fluffy coat removed, the meat cooked to perfection on a spit lit by a villager's own flame, the king's guardian and all round warrior savoured the taste of the meat as it slipped effortlessly down his throat, wondering if this was the way forward. It did seem finicky, to have to cook your prey all the time, but in his mind at least, the reward well outstripped the work involved. Knowing that he'd have to tell the king when he got back, momentarily he imagined magnificent kitchens being built, vendors across the capital roasting their wares, the exotic waft of brilliantly cooked meats filling the alleys and streets of the capital, making your stomach rumble just by walking past. Hmmm... just the thought of it had his gigantic light blue belly gurgling in anticipation. Abruptly, a tap on the shoulder startled him back to reality.

"Would you like some more?" offered Lil'th, Keesha's mother, having apparently heard his belly rumbling.

"That would be great, if it's not too much trouble," he replied, knowing that he'd need to be full when they started out on their return journey.

As he watched, two of the villagers pulled another hot, sizzling roasted lamb off the spit, and brought it over to where he sat on the sand.

"Thanks," he said, as they stabbed the bottom of the

spit into the ground, letting it just stand there like a donor kebab in a takeaway's window. As he started chomping on it wildly, his friend the librarian dropped to the floor beside him, chunks of much more raw meat and a selection of vegetables in the bowl that he was carrying.

"My friend," For'son announced, greeting him fondly, something which was almost a new experience for the both of them. "How's your day been?"

About to slide what looked like a whole leg of lamb down into his prehistoric jaw, Orac stopped and considered the question.

"Really good, thanks. As a matter of fact, I need to talk to you about the crystals."

"What about them?"

"I... I... I think they might be the key to sending messages around the world."

"WHAT?!" exclaimed the warrior, nearly choking on his food as he did so.

"What I said... I think the crystals have the power to help us transmit simple messages around the world, in... not quite the blink of an eye, but fast. If we could do that, imagine how easy it would be to keep in touch with other enclaves of dragons. There'd be no need for messengers, saving hundreds of thousands, if not millions, of hours of flight time. If somewhere needed help that only the capital could provide, think how quickly we could respond... to natural disasters, rogue dark magic users, or any sort of pandemic. This, if I'm correct, could change the face of the planet forever."

'Wow,' For'son thought, not entirely convinced of it as a concept, but sure that if Orac thought he could get it to work, then he had little doubt it would become the next big thing in the king's armoury to help the world at large. Wanting to assist in any way possible, he tried to predict where this was going.

"You want to take some of the crystals back to London?"

"I do. We harvested some earlier on today."

"We?"

"Keesha and I."

"Ohhh... nice!"

"How old are you?" the librarian asked sarcastically.

"One hundred and forty six, not that it's any of your business."

"Anyhow... we harvested as much as I thought we could carry, and have adapted some bags so that we can do just that."

"How much?" For'son asked, wanting to know about the extra weight, they, or more likely... he, was expected to lug.

"Ummm... quite a lot," answered Orac sheepishly, ironic considering what they were both eating.

"Is it really that important?"

Gulping down half a dozen tomatoes, a whole lettuce and half a cabbage, the repository guardian nodded frantically in response.

"We've got an awfully long way to go," For'son mused to no one in particular.

Immediately the look on the librarian's face changed to one more suited to a lost puppy than that of an apex predator, which was what he was supposed to be.

Shaking his head, knowing full well he was going to give in, he smiled at his friend and said they'd try and take it back, TRY being the optimal word.

And that was that. Orac had got his way regarding the crystals, and so they continued to enjoy their last night with the villagers, which included more of the fabulous food, the two friends consuming as much as their bellies would allow in preparation for their long journey, as well as singing, dancing (For'son most certainly didn't join in with this... Orac was reluctantly persuaded by, yes you can guess... Keesha, a dragon he was besotted with, one he'd do absolutely anything for) and much drinking, some of which included some kind of alcohol that was distilled from a vegetable called a potato, something the royal guardian gave short shrift to.

Piercing the darkness, the sun's first morning rays swept across their encampment, casting light and shadow in nearly equal amounts, the dragon villagers' slumber all but over, some of them looking more worse for wear than others, due in no small part to the happenings of the night before.

Awake immediately, For'son rechecked the bags that his friend had assembled, noting how the crystals had all been surrounded by linen and in some cases, straw.

'Clearly he's not taking any chances,' he thought. 'It must be important.' Ten minutes later, all ablutions taken care of, he returned to the bags only to find half of the village there to see them off.

Orac stepped forward, all the time holding Keesha's hand, something the librarian seemed both embarrassed and proud of in equal amounts.

"Keesha," said For'son, bowing his head in greeting.

"For'son," replied the exquisite golden dragon, bowing in return.

"It's time for us to leave I'm afraid Orac. Are you ready?" announced the king's protector, all business like.

"I am."

"Standing up tall, in front of all her friends and family, Keesha attempted to express the gratitude they all felt towards the pair of visitors from the capital.

"You've helped us so much. We can never repay the debt we owe you. If ever you or the king should need us, we will be there, rest assured of that. Our offer of friendship is always out there. And on a more personal level, if either of you ever want somewhere to holiday, you should know that you're always welcome here. We thank you for your bravery, courage and intelligence. Without you, we'd still be slaves to the ra-hoon, something I'm sure you both know. Have a safe journey, and we look forward to seeing you again sometime."

And with that, the stunning golden, yellow and orange dragon leaned in and kissed Orac directly on the mouth, much to his total and utter surprise. Pulling back, all the time smiling, Keesha and the others made room for the two of them to take off. Adding the weighty leather bags which were joined in the middle, akin to saddle bags, of which For'son's was about three times the size of Orac's, putting them gently across their backs, the two pals waved goodbye to all the villagers, and in one swift bound, leapt skyward, in the haze of the sun and now bright blue sky, both sorry to leave, but delighted to have made new lifelong friends.

It took them three stops and four and a half days to get back to the capital, London, during which time the bond between the two of them grew even stronger, For'son admitting to the librarian that he had had doubts about his participation in the mission, and that he'd been wrong to do so, knowing full well that he'd be dead right now if not for Orac, the crystals, Keesha and the other villagers. After which he'd said, much to the repository guardian's pleasure, there's no point in taking out five ra-hoon if you're killed by the sixth, something that seemed to sum up their previous predicament perfectly.

Making their way through the humdrum life of the buzzing capital, passing traders, architects, politicians and artisans, each noting how the size of the covered up statue had seemed to grow by a metre or so since their last visit, both dragons rocked up at the king's office, much to the monarch's pleasure.

"My friends, it's so great to have you back, and in one piece too," announced Greger, as pleased as punch, something that made both the librarian and warrior wary.

"Majesty," they both stated simultaneously, each bowing their head slightly.

"Now... there's no need for all of that, not while it's

just the three of us," replied the monarch, still full of cheer.

'What's going on?' wondered For'son, sure that something was up. But before he could ask, the king had a question.

"And how are our friends the ra-hoon? Put firmly in their place I do hope."

"Ripped them a new one," announced Orac, beating the warrior to it.

"Excellent! Did you encounter any problems?"

"Nothing we couldn't handle, sire," For'son answered, eager to move the subject on.

But the monarch didn't want to leave it at that.

"And how did you get on working together?"

"Fine," ventured the librarian.

"More than fine," added the protector. "It would seem that Orac and I make a pretty fair team and work well out in the field together. I'd like the chance to do that again some time."

"So would I," added the keeper of knowledge.

Sensing just how genuine they both were, Greger replied.

"I'm glad to hear it."

"And so what's been going on here while we've been away?" asked For'son, keen to understand exactly why his friend was so happy.

"You won't believe me when I tell," observed the king, all the time a glint in his eye.

"Go on."

"It's Ahrensburg... we've arranged to send a diplomatic delegation to their capital."

Both Orac and For'son's jaws hung wide open, unable to believe exactly what they were hearing.

"How...?" started the warrior protector, unable to believe just how much things had changed since he'd been gone.

"Through the help of a trusted backchannel who has

the ear of their ruler, Nev'dir. The talks themselves start in three days. The diplomatic delegations will be leaving tonight. A banquet is being thrown in their honour in two days."

"I'm... I'm... I'm gobsmacked and utterly amazed," said the blue shaded dragon, his mind still spinning. "I honestly thought, with everything we know about Nev'dir and his land that we'd have to use violence to rid him of his reign."

"I know my friend, I know. I thought the same, but this opportunity came right out of the blue, and is one that can't be ignored. If we can close the deal and get them to join our cause, we'll have done it, brought the world together, united as one. What an achievement."

"Congratulations, sire," added Orac, "it's a true victory for you and your vision of how life should be across the planet."

"Thank you, my friend, but let's not count our dragons before they've hatched. There's still work to be done, and the outcome is anything but assured."

"So who's leading the diplomatic delegation?" asked For'son, wondering which of their top dragons would take on such a mission.

"Well..." ventured the king, more than a little apprehensively, "the dragon that I've chosen will need to have a good understanding of what needs to be achieved, be as diplomatically correct as possible, but will need one important characteristic that few in the diplomatic corps have."

"And what's that?"

"To be able to smell a trap or know when they're being played."

"Good call. So who's the lucky chap?"

Swallowing uncomfortably, feeling a mixture of guilt and apprehension, especially given what his friend had already been through over the last month or so, Greger, knowing that there could be no beating around the bush, just blurted it out.

"It's you For'son. I'd like you to lead the diplomatic delegation to Ahrensburg."

If his jaw had hung open before, it nearly touched the ground now.

"Majesty?"

"I'm sorry my friend, I know it's not ideal, but I truly believe in my heart of hearts that you're the best qualified individual to lead the diplomatic delegation to the heart of Nev'dir's domain. While everything to do with the arrangements all look above board, there's always the chance of treachery and deceit. I've been assured by some of my best operatives that's not the case... but still, I find it hard to put my trust in a land, and more importantly a leader, that rules as he does."

Both Orac and For'son nodded at their leader's take on the situation.

"It brings me no great pleasure to ask this of you, and yes... I am asking. You can refuse if you want, and it won't be held against you in any way, shape or form. But I do believe you're eminently qualified to lead the diplomats there and keep them as safe as is possible. There's always a risk, more so this time than any other that I can recall, but if this works... we'll have united every dragon across the planet. Global peace will reign forever. Think of the possibilities, not just for dragonkind, but every species we share the world with. As you know, this has long been my goal and personal dream. I believe that it now lies almost within our grasp. Please, accept the assignment and finish what we've both started."

For a moment it was all too much to take in for the brave, blue shaded dragon, his mind still spinning from taking on the ra-hoon and the long flight back. But one thing and one thing only brought him back to reality with a bang, and that was his friendship with the king. He would literally do anything for him, that's how close they were, and although exhausted, and really not wanting to, there and then he put himself forward, just as the monarch knew he would do.

"I'll do it, sire. When do we leave?"

"Midnight... you should arrive at the outer reaches of their border sometime after sunrise tomorrow. After that, you'll be escorted to the capital, where hopefully you'll be able to bargain for their admission into our very large slice of the planet. Nothing's off the table, and I'm very happy for you to take your lead from our chief negotiator, Thomas, who'll be amongst those I'm sending with you. There'll be ten in all, far less than the usual amount that we'd send, but with good reason. If things progress well, then we can always send more. Be wary though, you know most of what has transpired on Nev'dir's watch and exactly what he's capable of. While this all looks legitimate, there is a chance that it's a double cross of some sort. How, or why, I really can't see, but that's not to say it's not there."

"Understood, sire," stated For'son.

"I'll go get my things ready and meet you at midnight," Orac chipped in all smiles.

"Ummm..." mused the monarch. "I'm afraid librarian that the group selected does not include you."

"But... but... but we worked so well together against the ra-hoon. I can be of use sire... honestly."

The king gave For'son a look, a kind of... do you want to tell him, or shall I?

"I'm sorry Orac, but there's no place for you on this one. Anything else, then I'd gladly have you along," observed the warrior, but there's just too much risk involved. If we're betrayed, and there's a slight chance we will be, then you'll be a liability. And before you start, I don't mean that disrespectfully. You've already proved your worth ten times over against the ra-hoon... but not this time. We're only taking a skeleton group as it is. Okay?"

Heartbroken and devastated at not being able to go on

another mission with his friend, the dejected repository guardian nodded his head in agreement, a sadder sight it was hard to think of.

"And don't forget," added the royal protector, "you've got other more important work to do."

That brightened up the librarian's face, something the king took note of and decided to enquire about, much to Orac's delight. Over the course of the next ten minutes or so, both dragons, one more than the other, clarified their exploits and explained the potential of the crystals. To say Greger was intrigued was something of an understatement. It finished, with the three of them going their separate ways, all vowing to meet up at midnight for a last farewell before the diplomatic delegation left, led by For'son.

It had been difficult to know what to take. Of course the journey was nowhere near the length of the one that he'd just come back from, the one in which he'd had to carry what felt like almost his own body weight in crystals thanks to his friend, but carrying anything at all would slow him down, hinder his excellent reflexes and could make him appear weak to those from the other side, watching him. After much reflection, well... about an hour, because they didn't actually have that much time, he choose a glinting silver blade, a scimitar in fact, from his collection that he'd picked up on his travels. After examining it in great detail, particularly the intricate gold weave around the perfectly formed hilt, he tucked it safely in its leather sheath and grabbing one of the long fleece robes from a pile nestled in the corner, said goodbye once again to his meagre quarters, only then realising just how little he'd been here over the last two or three years. Smack bang out of the blue, it hit him right between the eyes. He didn't want to go. Not to complete the mission... no! He wanted to stay here, have a shot at some kind of life, forge new friendships, cement the current ones with Orac and Greger, maybe even find the right mate to have a family with. Staring out of the thick, rattling glass window which afforded him a view of the stars, momentarily he wondered if what he sought was possible. He'd lived a life on the edge for so long, combat and battle all he could ever remember knowing, and now this... they were on the verge of planet wide peace. What an opportunity. But how would he fare once it was all over? Would the world accept someone of his ilk? Would his particular set of skills make him all but redundant? Would he just be put out to pasture like a hobbled old horse, with no say, no role to play? Never before had any of these thoughts or feelings troubled him or raised their ugly heads. Why now? Was it because of the mission he was about to go on, or was it related to their assignment with the ra-hoon? Briefly he considered both, but could draw no firm conclusion. Perhaps it was just Fate, giving him a little nudge in the right direction or a glimpse into his future. Either way, he had no time for that now. Shoving the huge fleece into a gigantic brown leather bag that he knew he could carry all the way there, he said goodbye to his room and his few measly belongings and, closing the door behind him, headed for the outer fortifications of the city, to meet up with the other members of the delegation he'd be leading to Ahrensburg.

Under a cloudless, moonlit sky and against the sound of the crackling and spitting orange and yellow torches, the delegation of diplomats, having introduced themselves to For'son, including Thomas, the chief negotiator, whose advice he'd rely on wholeheartedly, strolled over in a line and shook the king's outstretched hand, the monarch conveying just what an important mission they were about to set out on, telling them how proud he was of each and every one of them. And then it was For'son's turn to address his friend and monarch.

Reaching out as he had done hundreds of times before, he clasped the cold scaled hand, relishing the comfort and normality of it all, leaving it locked for far longer than was customary.

"Everything okay?" Greger asked, noting the discrepancy in time.

"No," For'son replied, pulling his hand back next to the bright blue brilliant wings tucked in by his side.

"You don't have to go. Even now there's a contingency."

"It's okay... I'll be fine. I guess I'll just be glad when this is all over and peace reigns across the land."

"Amen to that," mused the king. "You'll be back soon, and who knows, maybe in a couple of months this will all be cleared up and we'll be able to sit down and put our feet up."

"That would be good," announced the warrior, about to turn diplomat.

"Good hunting," ventured the monarch, offering up the lines to the private joke that only the two of them understood.

"To us all," replied his friend, the scimitar firmly in its sheath strapped to his back, as well as the bag containing the fleece that no doubt he would need, given the much colder conditions where they were going.

Suddenly the two of them were alerted to the plodding of footsteps pounding on stone, accompanied by some serious heavy breathing, something even the best nuisance caller would be proud of.

"Orac... you made it," bellowed For'son, wrapping his much bigger wings and frame around the squat little librarian, encompassing him almost fully.

Momentarily hidden from sight, the cunning repository guardian used his exquisite sleight of hand to slip something tiny into the hidden pouch around his friend's waist before they stepped apart from one another.

"I wouldn't miss it for the world... friend."

The two of them were unlikely allies, let alone best friends, but that's what they'd become, and shook each other's hands, much as the warrior had just done with the king. But there was something different about it this time, a familiarity that the two of them had become comfortable with, something the king was proud of, looking on, from off to one side.

"How are you getting on with the crystals?"

"I've done a few rudimentary tests, all of which seem very positive. I'm looking forward to investigating them in even more depth."

"Well... hopefully by the time I return, you'll have done just that and be well on your way to providing us with worldwide communications."

"Steady on," replied the librarian. "Currently it's only a theory, a promising one I grant you, but that's all that it is."

"I know, I'm only kidding. You take care of yourself... and I'll see you in a week or so and we'll catch up properly and you can tell me all about the crystals."

"Sounds good... take care."

"Always," replied For'son.

And with that, he gave them both a nod and strolled over to the gathered diplomats who were all ready and waiting.

Without so much as looking back, they, as a group, all bounded into the air, circling ever skyward over the fortifications of the capital, creating a huge dragon spiral, before eventually they all banked sharply and against the backdrop of only the whistling wind, headed north in the direction of... Ahrensburg.

For the most part, they stuck to flying over land, that is until there was no more, some of them relishing the salty spray from the crashing waves, others preferring to fly much higher up, taking advantage of the huge updrafts and friendly winds, allowing them to expend less energy. As a group, they made good progress, but there was no rush, they had plenty of time before they were due at the border of the two lands to meet their assigned escorts.

During the course of their flight, the temperature dropped significantly, with all of them having, in some small part, to use the magic that was their birthright to keep themselves warm. Various mantras on a theme were enacted, some igniting a shield atop their scales, deflecting the biting cold, others using the supernatural to send warmth coursing through their veins to the outlying regions of their huge prehistoric bodies, all effectively keeping themselves alive, because the cold itself is a dragon's worst nightmare, and can without warning slow their minds, freeze their scales, prevent them from taking flight, or dampen down their ethereal energy and extinguish the flame that sits at the base of their belly which some think is intrinsically linked to their very soul. So venturing into a land that was renowned across the world for just how chilly it could get was not only full of diplomatic pitfalls, but very real physical dangers, something all the members of the group were well aware of, in particularly their brave and courageous leader, the stunningly shaded blue dragon, that even as they travelled, attempted to run every scenario, both good and bad, through his mind with a view to systematically pulling it apart, piece by piece, on the lookout for anything that could go wrong or any sign of treachery. The other dragons with him, he knew, were his responsibility, and he was determined to do everything in his power to keep them safe. And so as the monotony of the darkness and the water continued, his brilliant and unconventional mind continued to scour options and possibilities in an effort to foresee anything that could go wrong. But would it be enough, and could he predict any future outcome? Read on to find out.

Hours later as the scattered rays of the sun started to burst through the grey and white fluffy clouds, lighting up the sky and their way forward, landfall was spotted by one of their group, the scenery much more dynamic and harsh than that which they were accustomed to. Skirting archipelagos, following the detailed instructions they'd been given, they traversed the angry grey and black shadowed seas, soaring over magnificent snow covered fjords, against a backdrop of gigantic ice capped mountains. It was both awe inspiring and terrifying to every member of the delegation, and a timely reminder that they were far away from home and everything they found familiar and comforting.

Reaching a monumental frozen fjord that appeared to be at least two miles wide, at the end of a body of water, For'son, now in the lead of their compact group, banked hard right, heading for a gap in the mountains, as reassured as he could be by the daylight, his eidetic memory having perfectly stored the directions they'd been given by the backchannel source that had supposedly set this all up. Pushing on, now remaining at altitude, something that had advantages and disadvantages, the small group of primeval monsters hissed through the air, almost cutting through the very molecules themselves, their unfamiliar surroundings prompting them to focus even more on the mission, reinforcing the danger they were facing. Professionals, all of them, they stuck to their formation, all the time on the lookout for anything unusual, and followed their leader into the belly of the beast.

As the middle of the day arrived, so did they, rounding yet another dark, dismal uninviting lake, plunging over the side of a two hundred metre cliff face, dropping down onto a terminal moraine, the edge of a glacier, marking the point of its maximum advance. Both beautiful and deadly, to a dragon at least, on touching down on the rocky beach, each of them took a moment to catch their breath and admire the view. None of them had ever seen anything like it.

"We're early by the looks of things," stated Harold through their telepathic group link. He was one of the diplomats who specialised in the detail of law and anything pertaining to it.

"Just how I like it," replied For'son, gazing around for anything that could be a trap.

"How long do you think we'll have to wait for them to arrive?" asked Thomas out loud, without the buffeting winds, sure there was no one else in listening range.

As if to answer his question, suddenly out of nowhere, a huge dark blob appeared on the horizon against the cloudy sky which was now more white than grey, the anger, at least for the time being, seeming to have disappeared.

"It looks, my friend, as though you have your answer," the shaded blue warrior announced, pointing out the fast moving swirl of darkness with the tip of his right wing, that even with their magically enhanced senses, they still couldn't see in any great detail.

"Whatever that is, it's moving at quite some rate," exclaimed Fanti, the youngest of them all at a mere hundred years, a beautiful green and brown example of their race, tiny in size, well... compared with their leader at least, but what she lacked there, she more than made up for in intelligence and the art of diplomacy.

And she was right... it was... way too fast, as far as For'son was concerned, to land even vaguely safely amongst any of them. Was it a trap, he wondered. Could it be a test of their steel perhaps, or something else, a traditional greeting for strangers entering their kingdom for the first time? Knowing that at times like this you HAD to hold your nerve, he focused in on the fast moving objects, urged those around him to calm down through their shared link, and waited to see exactly what would happen next.

Heading for their exact position at what could only be described as high speed, the dark coloured blurs cut through the air, close enough now for the diplomatic delegation to see each individual. Ten... that's how many there were in all, each one resembling something out of any creature's worst nightmare. Fanti gasped, having never seen anything so horrific and terrifying. She wasn't the only one. For'son, having suspected something like this swallowed nervously, the only telltale sign that he was anything but ready. By now he'd run this scenario through his mind, and having been briefed on just how ungodly some of the beings they were dealing with could not only be, but look, especially from what he'd been told, their leader, deep inside his mind, continued to tell himself not to judge a tome by its cover, in the hope that the new arrivals would at least be educated enough and polite enough to grant them safe passage. If not... then this would all be over in a heartbeat.

Baring down on them now, still carrying all their built up forward momentum, teeth exposed, their savage physiques showing off bulging muscles and a multitude of scars and wounds from previous encounters, at the very last moment the monsters of this land sent to greet them opened out their wings, brought their tails forward almost simultaneously, and crashed to the rocky ground feet first with an almighty THUMP, that reverberated out across the ice-like beach they found themselves on, the concussion wave nearly knocking For'son's group off their feet.

'Designed to intimidate,' thought the blue shaded warrior, aware of nearly all the tricks of the trade, having used most over the last four decades whilst serving his friend the king in an effort to unite all of the world's lands in an attempt to bring peace to everyone. With that in mind, deep inside his head he urged himself to calm down and not react with anything less than a kind and polite attitude.

Dwarfing every dragon there, a huge, dark brown monster of a beast stomped forwards across the pebbled beach, stone, sand and rubble kicking up from around his feet and talons as he moved, a collection of scars adorning his chest and chin, some of which were clearly fresh... no more than a few days old at best. That however, wasn't the most fear inducing thing, and neither was the necklace of yellowy-white dragon's teeth that circled his neck. No! That was reserved for his eyes... or more specifically his left eye, which, if they'd had to guess, was missing, because a huge, black, metallic plate hung over where it should have been, very much resembling a pirate's eye patch, evidently fused to the scale and bone surrounding the socket. At the very sight of this, a touch of fear ran through all those dispatched by the king, including his best friend who, in all his travels, had never seen anything quite like it.

Towering over all of them, the monster approached, encroaching deeply into For'son's personal space, glaring down at him as though he were something insignificant to be played with, or a trapped item of prey. Holding his ground, the valiant leader waited for the beast to speak, aware of the intricacies of diplomacy surrounding first contact, knowing that any kind of breach of protocol could end things faster than a rip-roaring fart on a first date. Taking them all in from his great height, the huge primeval fiend sniffed the air, seemingly offended by their scent. Still all of them held their ground, Fanti by now a quivering wreck inside, but intelligent and brave enough not to show it in her outward appearance.

Craning his neck down to look For'son directly in the face, their noses only a matter of inches apart, the disgusting smell of his maggot infested jaw assaulting the king's friend's olfactory senses to the point of wanting to retch. Only then did the fear inducing dark dragon speak.

"This is what they sent, a puny, pathetic group of dragons who look like they couldn't catch their own lunch, let alone pose a threat to any of their own kind," goaded the fiend.

What happened next was totally unexpected. The monster of a beast spat in disgust, straight onto the middle of For'son's bright blue chest, the thick foamy bile sticking in a huge white blob.

Every single atom inside him raged, the bloodlust

within practically burning, desperate to find a way out and exact revenge for the despicable and disrespectful deed. Despite the fury and anger deep down, he remained calm, at least outwardly, absolutely sure this was some kind of trial, one there was no way in hell he was going to react to. And so he did what he knew would annoy them most... he looked him straight in the eye and continued to smile.

As all of the other diplomats from the south looked on in a mixture of utter terror and deep fascination, it was almost possible to see the vehemence and fury roil off the one-eyed monster, his muscles tense, ready to fight, his teeth exposed, sure that he could take down the much smaller dragon he faced.

Full of his usual cunning and guile, worried only because there were other lives at stake rather than just his, the king's friend and mighty warrior assessed the situation.

'Clearly,' he thought, 'this one wants to fight, but is it part of the ritual, something to prove his worth, or is this all part of their leader's plan, to keep us off guard and see what we're made of?'

Pulling a deep breath in through his nostrils, not for one second taking his eyes off the mountainous, shadowy dragon before him, For'son found the cold, dark, selfish centre that was the warrior deep inside, and pushing any other thoughts aside, readied himself for what would come. He didn't have to wait very long.

The capital's library, a work in progress, had for the most part been converted into a makeshift workshop. Books, tomes and scrolls with tiny ribbons of all colours holding them together had been either piled up high, or scattered across the floor, mainly accumulating in the much colder, darker corners of the huge rooms, something that was unusual in itself, because the guardian of the repository, Orac, nearly always took good care of what he thought of as his charges, showing them more love than he ever did himself.

Across two colossal oak tables sat a vast array of crystals, grouped together by colour, and then sorted into length. There must have been two thousand in all, if you included some of those on the floor, still left to be sorted.

Weary, still aching from the return journey, the dedicated librarian stopped what he was doing and momentarily wondered what both his new found friends were up to. Keesha he was sure would be knee deep in work, no doubt helping the villagers and her friends with the everyday chores of life. As if by magic, and that might well have had something to do with it, a perfect rendition of her smiling face appeared right at the front of his mind, sending a shiver up his squat little tail and goose bumps down both arms, whilst his stomach rolled and rallied. Briefly, but only that, his mind wondered what on earth all those bizarre feelings were. You and I would know, but for poor Orac it was different. He had absolutely no clue.

Pushing aside everything unusual happening to his intricately scaled form, his thoughts turned to his friend, wondering exactly what he was up to, hoping he was safe, eager for him to return so that they could spend some more time together, whether in the makeshift library that both of them had put so much effort into setting up, or out on another daring and dangerous mission.

Speaking of which...

Turning away, feigning disinterest, the monstrous dragon, as quick as a flash, pivoted on one foot, bringing his other leg around in a spinning blur of a roundhouse kick, exactly at For'son's head height. Had it made contact, it probably would have been the end for the brave warrior. However, he was the royal protector for many reasons, one of them being his fighting prowess and lightning fast reactions. And so as the prehistoric dark foot sliced through the air, razor sharp, dirty yellow talons edging out as far as they'd go, meant to cleave his opponent's head from his body, For'son rolled off to the right, coming up out of range of his attacker, watching every movement, waiting to see not only how his adversary would react next, but more importantly, whether or not the rest of his entourage would attempt to take on the diplomats that he was responsible for. Luckily, the answer to that was no, every other being there preferring to stand still and watch the outcome of the initiated personal battle.

More than a little peeved about the strange turn of events that had led to them both fighting, For'son had little time to dwell on that now, because with the roundhouse kick avoided, the dark beast stumbled back to his feet, enraged that the focus of his ire had escaped what he'd thought of as an exquisite attack, and with fury bubbling off him and murder in his eyes, he surged forward in one all out attack.

Milliseconds, that's how long it took for the diplomatic leader to assess the situation he found himself in, and more importantly, the threat posed by his opponent.

Throwing the sheath containing his glistening silver scimitar to the ground along with the saddle bag containing the fleece, knowing that it would only restrict his movements and might actually get him killed, his ever agile mind pondered the situation.

'Fast,' he thought, 'with good reactions, which of course doesn't bode well, but he was quick to anger and with him being blinded on one side by the ridiculous metal plate over his left eye, which might prove to be his undoing. Of course magic hasn't come into play yet... which seems odd. Perhaps that's against the rules, if indeed there are such things.' Wondering if that were the case, and knowing that to break such a covenant would be an awful faux pas that might well end negotiations before they'd even started, the brilliantly blue shaded dragon decided to reserve his magic and wait to see if the brutal beast rushing towards him would use it first. If this was going to be an all out physical fight he could cope with that, despite his attacker having a huge weight and height advantage.

Surging forward, wings outstretched, jaws wide open, needle sharp teeth bared, ready to bite down, the massive monster missed his target by only a few millimetres, that's how close it had been. Diving off to one side, before rolling twice in quick succession to put a little bit of space between the two of them, For'son now struggled to contain the blistering rage that was building up inside him. Nobody had mentioned this would be a part of things... if they had, he might have reconsidered. Of course he wouldn't have, willing to do anything for his pal the king, but it would have been nice to know exactly what he was getting himself into.

'And who's to say,' he thought, 'that the others won't join in if I succeed in taking this one down? What to do, what to do?'

Blinded by rage, gripped by his unforgiving temper, deep within he fumed as the blue dragon that was supposedly their leader once again escaped his clutches, running away just before he could get his hands, or more likely his teeth on him. Deciding that the pathetic excuse for a dragon must be some kind of cowardly, career diplomat, not trained in the art of battle, this one thought spurred him on even more, should such a thing be possible, determined as he was to obey his leader's commands and make them suffer a despicable blow before negotiations had even begun. It was a shame he didn't recognise a worthy opponent when he saw one, because if he had, it might just have saved him a world of pain and misery.

'It's time,' thought the king's friend, knowing that the seriousness of the situation and its lethality had increased tenfold over the last few seconds. With only one real choice, if he wanted to keep the others he was responsible for out of it, he bent his knees, the brilliant bright bulging blue muscles in his thighs straining, the sinew almost visible through his scales, and with one almighty bound, he leapt straight into the air, flapping his wings furiously looking to gain as much height as he could in an effort to put some distance between him and the rest of the group.

Sure that he now had the puny little weakling on the run and scared for his life, Chillblade, as that was his name, quickly followed suit, shooting straight up from the rock strewn beach they found themselves on, his humungous wings powering him through the air, adeptly defying gravity, all the time closing in on the object of his ire that had escaped him twice already. Clouded by dark thoughts, of one thing he was sure... it wouldn't happen a third time.

Easing up a little so as to make it look as though he were tiring, For'son took a long, deep breath, soaked in the feeling of the cold, crisp, pure air, and recognising that he had absolutely no choice in the matter, slipped seamlessly into battle mode, knowing now that it was do or die. And this was when he came into his own.

Beating his wings hard and fast, sweat soaking his face and dripping down past the dark metal eye patch that was fused to the scales and bone of his skull, before he'd even got within range, the wicked dark monstrosity already knew what he was going to do: bite through one of the petrified little dragon's wings, stopping it from fleeing, before chomping down on one of its tasty looking legs. That's right, in the land of Ahrensburg, it wasn't uncommon for those that had the leader's ear and trust to be cannibals, often consuming their enemies and those that were deemed to have lost faith in their ruler. Twisted, uncompromising, dark, devious, demonic, outrageous and desperately undemocratic were all words that could very accurately describe just some of the things that those in charge of this land were capable of.

Almost ground to a halt now, hovering high up in the cloud speckled sky, For'son knew that he made a tempting target, especially for this half witted loon that had absolutely no idea what he was facing. Pretty soon he'd find out.

Wings pumping furiously, the whole of his body one speeding blur, Chillblade rocketed up from underneath, knowing that the frightened little dragon had no idea he was approaching in his blind spot. In a moment or two, he'd have him.

Fully aware of the situation, his magical senses stretched out as far as they could go, For'son waited until the very last moment to make his move. Flipping himself backwards with everything he had, he rolled, tucked in, extended his talons as far as possible, and as the monstrous black blur streaked past him, missing his intended target by less than half a metre, the brave and courageous royal protector raked him down his thick muscled tail, brilliant tears of thick green blood splashing out into the sky, dropping precariously towards the ground.

Astounded that anything could move that fast, before he knew it an excruciating pain blossomed out of his tail, causing him to shriek in absolute agony and spiral off to one side. For most, what had happened would signal the need for caution, but the dark dragon envoy was too far gone to care about any of that, the basest bloodlust built into his DNA gripping him for all he was worth.

Clinging on to the hope that one strike might just do it and that they could return to the ground and resume their diplomatic personas, it was evident straight away, at least to For'son, in no small part from the loud snarl and the body language of his adversary, that this was far from over.

'DAMN!' thought the king's friend, wanting to do anything but fight. It appeared though that the choice had been well and truly taken out of his hands.

Pissed at missing his prey, his confidence not so much shattered as hanging by a thread, Chillblade slammed his tail upwards, which given the damage done caused a ripple of mind numbing agony to roll up his entire body, extended both shadowy wings out as far as they'd go and momentarily glided to a halt, his mind and body filled with more hatred and anger than it had ever known, and given just who he was, how he'd reached the position he had, and the land that he lived in, was saying quite something. Being bested by a dragon half his size was one thing, but in front of the others that had accompanied him here was something else all together. Determined to right a vicious wrong he arched his neck, darted down and closing fast, prepared himself for one all out head-on-attack.

'Oh crap,' was all For'son had time to think, caught by surprise by the blunt, reckless and frankly outdated tactics the beast he'd already beaten once had decided to employ. Pinwheeling off to one side, For'son lurched off to the left and then pitched down, hoping to avoid the violent and forthright confrontation, knowing that because they were so outmatched he'd be the one to take the brunt of it. Unfortunately, despite his cat-like reflexes, he was just a fraction of a second too late, the dark fiery fiend slamming into his right shoulder, sending him into the mother of all flat spins, momentarily disorientating him, his wings and tail of little use, the clouds and horizon zipping past at an unerring rate, the pain from his aching shoulder pounding his mind into submission. Wildly out of control, lost and lonely, it really did look as though, for once, he might have bitten off more than he could chew.

On the ground, through their shared telepathic link, the diplomatic contingent expressed their concern at what was happening.

"We have to do something," urged Fanti, her enthusiasm and worry shining through.

"I really don't think that's an option," said Musim, a tall, thin, graceful dragon, dotted with dappled yellow and red blotches, and behind Thomas, the most experienced of the group. *"We have to let it play out and hope that he can turn the tables. Whether he does or not, none of this bodes well for what lies ahead."*

"Give him a chance," Ecoack went on, a middle sized,

perfectly formed plum coloured dragon with just a hint of white outlining the outer edges of her sumptuous scaled face.

"Agreed," added Francis, another of their group. *"He'll come through, I just know it."*

"Enough chatter," announced Thomas, all business-like, wanting no distractions, aware that it might not only be For'son's fate that depended on the outcome of the aerial duel.

Antediluvian faces all glued to the sky, as one they wished their leader well, sending their encouragement through the link, hoping that he'd not only be aware of it, but that he could use it to his advantage.

Unfortunately he couldn't feel a thing, at least not mentally, because his concentration was elsewhere right now, trying not to throw up. Now you might think that dragons were immune to high G forces, wild spins and precarious drops, and to some extent you'd be right, but what was happening now was unlike anything the king's friend had ever experienced. He was spinning so fast it was impossible for those watching below, even with their enhanced supernatural senses, to distinguish his tail from his head, and For'son was one almighty blue blur, which had now started to drop like a stone. That was the only thing keeping him out of the mouth the cruel and vicious Chillblade.

Doubling back on himself after clattering into the very naive and stupid diplomat of those coveting their land, the one eyed brute of a dragon considered his options. Sure that his opponent was going to crash heavily into the thick sea of ice below, death seemed inevitable because of the height he'd come down from and the speed he was travelling, a realisation that had Chillblade smiling inside. Instantly that was curtailed because it then dawned on him what those looking on would think, and more importantly, report back to their leader. So harnessing all the rage and injustice that he felt at the blue dragon lasting so long and avoiding one of his signature attacks, he harnessed gravity and plunged towards the floor, desperate to get in a killing blow before the icy ground, and for Fate to add the finishing touches to what he'd started, all in an effort to show his cohorts exactly who was the boss.

Belching unceremoniously whilst spinning at a dizzying rate did little to regain For'son's composure. It did however relieve the need to throw up, for now at least... A small win, but one he'd take at the moment. Using all his mental will to ignore the G forces pummelling his reinforced primeval skull, his skilful intellect could only come up with one solution to his current predicament... MAGIC! But by now, the ground was swimming into view rather quickly, with little time to select any mantra, let alone the right one. And so in the gamble of his life, he used the most recent and familiar one, hoping against hope that it would be enough. Adding all his considerable willpower, and aiming towards the ice covered fjord that he was closing in on fast, he said the words, applied his ethereal energy and let the supernatural run riot.

It felt different this time, whether because of how out of control he was, the fact that he'd given all of himself over to it, or maybe, he thought, feeling more than a little nervous, perhaps he'd cast it wrong. If it were the latter, he'd be dead in a moment or two. The forking, arcing lightning had changed colour, alternating between fluorescent pink and a cool, dark purple, splitting the air with a series of constant low pitched BOOMS, underscored by a vicious crackling and hissing and the feel of the molecules themselves getting heavier. Drilling into the thick, white layer of ice that looked like a frozen sea retreating on the tide, the ignited air sent shattered fragments scattering in every direction as a series of mini explosions tore apart the fjord below For'son, a roiling, boiling cloud of steam enveloping everything, including the blue shaded warrior himself momentarily.

Plunging after his prey at breakneck speed in the

sharpest of dives, for an instant Chillblade lost sight of his target, as the thick, steamy white cloud of superheated water vapour spread out below. Sure that he was on the right track, he poured on as much velocity as he could, determined to end the wretched beast's life before the ground could do it for him, ready to reverse his body and use the razor sharp talons that had killed so many times before to 'slice and dice' as he liked to think of it. Doing just that, knowing that the ground was only metres away now, certain that his target would present itself through the thick fog that obscured his vision completely, he knew that the hunger within him was about to be satisfied by yet one more kill, the latest in a series that numbered in the hundreds over the last ten years alone.

Filthy yellow razor sharp talons outstretched, Chillblade arched his legs, his powerful thigh muscles as taut as they'd go, and waited for the gratifying feel of scale and sinew being ripped apart, his wings now outspread, burning off just some of the speed.

What would become a defining phrase for physicists everywhere some twenty thousand years or so later, could most certainly be applied in this instance. Every action has an equal and opposite reaction, the lightning surging out of him into the ground, slowing his descent, until he rather uncomfortably and clumsily landed feet first on top of the ice, a deadly ripple of dangerous forked cracks spreading out in all directions, with him at its centre. Taking a split second to appreciate how lucky he was to still be alive, engulfed in the thick, misty cloud of steam that currently felt like heaven, it was only then that For'son's sense of danger kicked in, having been too panicked and in too much of a spin to take note of his attacker heading after him. Really not wanting to, and knowing that the cold would pierce his body like a thousand puncturing needles all at the same time, the royal protector could see no other way out, and so without delay, he leapt off to one side and tumbling head over heels (not easy for a dragon to do), rolled over and over and over, putting at least fifty metres between himself and the spot where he'd landed. And that was probably the first break he'd gotten since this whole thing started because as he awkwardly staggered to his feet, his pursuer hit the ice HARD, in that exact same landing spot.

BOOM! Having misjudged where the ice of the fjord began, fully expecting to feel the tearing of plump dragon flesh and scale beneath his dirty yellow talons, Chillblade's whole body felt the impact with the slippery ground, a bone shaking rattle running up his primeval body, jolting his knees and back, his filthy teeth ringing like church bells, the agony absolutely exquisite.

Not usually one to take pleasure in another's pain, the bright blue leader of the diplomatic delegation from the south felt a pang of satisfaction watching the dark dragon smash so brutally into the ground, figuring he'd got his just deserts, hoping that would be enough and that they could all now get back to politics; after all, that was the whole reason they were here. Unfortunately, it was never going to be that simple.

Compelled by his leader's orders, with them feeling like a collar around his thick, dark, scaly neck, Chillblade fought off the pain from his unqualified landing and rose to his feet, spotting his prey through the clearing steam, just off to the side, looking intact and a little smug, something that riled him even more, if such a thing were possible. As the anger inside him took over, he roared the most heart stopping vicious roar of his life, and intent on having revenge for being made to look a fool, at least in his eyes, he bounded forth over the ice, flapping his two giant wings low to the ground in an effort to gain as much momentum as possible in his haste to reach For'son.

With his attacker almost on him once again, the king's friend had little time to react. Fortunately his battle trained mind instinctively commanded his body, forcing him up into the air and out of immediate danger before he'd even had a chance to realise exactly what had happened. After that, a decision was made.

Right or wrongly, he'd held his magic in check up until this point thinking that to do so was part of some unwritten code or diplomatic policy. But he'd had enough of whatever was going on, and in a decision that he knew might have huge ramifications, he allowed his ethereal energy to flood through him, one thought alone at the front of his mind: be damned with the consequences.

Almost ready to pounce, once again he watched his cowardly prey streak up into the sky just out of reach, making him angrier than Bruce Banner's alter ego. Stretching out both wings and lowering his centre of gravity, he drew to a halt, his sensitive feet burning from contact with the ice, something he pushed to the back of his mind, determined to end this as quickly as possible. In a fit of rage, and ignoring what should have been protocol, resolutely he followed the dastardly orders of his leader, in his case certainly not a friend, just another being in his way, and he knew if he didn't get this right, he'd be done for. I'm not talking about being demoted or punished, he'd simply be... DEAD! That was the plain truth of the matter. And so with his life on the line, he belched up a couple of huge fireballs in a row, spitting them out in his adversary's direction, and bounding into the air after them in one single leap, brought forth the most vicious of his magic, even though he knew he shouldn't have.

About to unleash some of his supernatural brilliance, instantly he was caught off guard as two flame dripping fireballs resembling tiny suns, brilliant bright yellow at their centres, surrounded by orange, red and blue licks of flame on the outside, came hurtling his way, their fiery tails making them look like explosive comets. Flipping upside down, defying gravity, he rolled over upon himself as the flaming projectiles flashed past, their heat scorching his wings, the pain from which kicked him into action. Jinking all the time, he sprinted towards the ice at a dizzying rate, pulling up at the last moment, skimming just a few centimetres above the dull, reflective surface, a cold, ice field cloud spiralling up in his wake.

Madness having almost fully taken over now, Chillblade had done the one thing all battle hardened beings are warned against doing when they're trained... he'd lost control. Not only of the situation, but of himself and his emotions, determined as he was to take down the shaded blue dragon no matter what the cost, the stark realisation that it was either that or be killed hitting him like a lumberjack's axe burying itself into the trunk of a tree.

Doubling back in the tightest turn possible, he swooped down onto his opponent's tail as debris in the form of rocks, stones and shards of pointed ice peppered his face. Ignoring all these whilst flying as close as he could, in his mind, he opted for one of his most vicious mantras, knowing that it would all be over in only a matter of moments.

Recognising the familiar touch deep inside his well balanced psyche, the royal protector and warrior instantaneously spoke the spell they'd all discovered on their last mission, used to protect them from the ra-hoon. Right here, right now, it saved his life, preventing Chillblade from mashing his brain from within, something that only stoked the dark dragon's rage and frustration.

'Impossible,' he thought. 'No being has ever managed to resist that particular mantra. What in the hell is going on?'

Sweat dribbling down his spine, despite the chilly conditions, For'son knew that it was time to turn the tables and take this bully down. For good or bad, he just couldn't allow this to go on much longer. How their leader would view this was anyone's guess.

In a series of frantic manoeuvres that had him sweeping past the frozen sea's breakers and up onto the pointed rocky coast on the far side of the fjord, only then did he remember his friend the king's cunning ploy back over the forest not so long ago, the one that had whittled down the number of pursuers and had allowed him to enter the cave below the rocky overhang, the one which he'd helped collapse. Reaching out with his mind, the demonic, murderous looking dark monster almost clinging to his tail in his slipstream, he lurched this way and that as more fireballs with a fierce intensity came scorching past, missing his wings and head by less than a gnat's genitalia. Knowing that it was now or never, opening a tiny hole in the defences surrounding his mind, he allowed the supernatural within him to leak out and find its target. No... not the revenge filled hunter firmly on his tail, but the huge jagged boulders over which they both flew. With a few selected just in front of his whistling form, inside he whispered the words, let the magic within him flow and, barrel rolling this way and that, gave over all the will he could spare.

Close now, almost able to chomp down on the tip of the brilliant blue tail in front of him, ignoring the pain from the debris flying up in his opponent's wake, the dark dragon, Chillblade, almost admired the guile of the opponent ahead of him as he opened his huge prehistoric jaws, ready to bite down and bring things to a conclusion. Distracted by this thought, revelling in potential glory, having taken his eye off the ball, he never saw it coming.

Below them, the ground quaked and rumbled as spiky boulders the size of cars broke apart at their base, half a dozen quivering as they did so. As the blistering fast blue blur cruised over them, like rockets leaving Cape Canaveral, they blasted into the air, missing For'son by a hair's breadth, skewering his dull witted shadow through his belly, both wings and tail.

As thick, brilliant green dragon blood splattered throughout the air, a shrill, piercing scream echoed across the ice and rock, one so loud and so bone chillingly terrifying, that it could only signify one thing... DEATH!

And that of a dragon. With an almighty THUD, Chillblade's body fused with the boulders that had acted like missiles and taken him down, smashed to the ground, and all the time gathering momentum, rolled down the side of the rocks and fell atop the frozen fjord, burying itself into the ice, only the tip of the improvised projectiles, one wing and his snout remaining showing. A more brutally sad sight it would have been harder to find.

Swishing his tail hard to the right, For'son banked back towards the two groups of opposing diplomats and pumping his wings, headed directly for them, magic surging through the whole of his monstrous, dinosaur-like body, ready to do battle should those from this land deem it necessary. Sending stones skittering in every direction, he landed with a bump between both factions, ethereal energy visible in shades of green and blue atop his fingertips, waiting to come into being, ready to be unleashed at a moment's notice, should the need arise. Thankfully though, it didn't appear to be the case, the diplomats from the other side looking more disinterested than anything else, one or two seemingly almost joyous at the demise of their colleague.

Studying his fingernails matter-of-factly, one of the others, now supposedly their leader, turned to face For'son, not bothered at all about what had happened, or the magic clearly visible in front of him.

"That," he said, "was most unfortunate. My understanding was that we were supposed to just guide you back to the capital and nothing else. You have my sincerest apologies."

"BULLSHIT!" spat Fanti through their shared group link, surprising them all.

"Calm down," urged their leader, the king's warrior friend, doing his best to follow his own advice. *"Getting angry now will not serve us well. They seem nonchalant about their comrade's death which could be for any number of reasons. Perhaps he went rogue or maybe he was just following orders. Either way,*

we'll probably never know. I suggest we follow their lead for the time being, but now you know the seriousness of the situation we all find ourselves in. There can be no turning back. For good or bad, we're here now and have to make the best of it. Stay alert. If you see or sense anything unusual, tell me immediately. Good luck."

With that he cut off communication, returning to the conversation with their diplomatic opposition.

Taking a long, deep breath in through his enormous nostrils, tiny licks of bright yellow flame sparkling out of each, and out through his humungous prehistoric jaw, he set about moving things along.

"What's supposed to happen next?" he asked, in a calm and controlled manner, the magic that had been so prominent atop his fingers tucked away for the moment.

"We'll escort you to the capital where, right at this very moment, a huge feast in your honour is being prepared. After that, you'll sit down with our leader to try and thrash out some sort of agreement. He's harsh but fair. You should have no trouble coming to an arrangement that suits you both."

'That,' thought For'son, 'doesn't sound entirely unreasonable.' He was still troubled though. Had it been any other land, any other beings but those here, and the despicable leader who he knew only a little about, but what he did turned his blood cold, then he might just have taken those words at face value. But he just couldn't, not with so much at stake, not only the lives of the other diplomats that had accompanied him here, but also peace for the whole planet, especially those living under the tyranny and threats of violence who needed to be free as quickly as possible. With all of that in mind, the blue shaded dragon strolled over to pick up his discarded scimitar and fleece.

"You won't be needing those or anything else," declared the de facto leader of the other side. "In fact you won't be needing anything. Leave all of your equipment here."

Knowing full well that it wasn't a request, For'son told

them through the link to put all their belongings on the ground, something they did immediately, each disappointed to have done so. After a little nod in recognition of what they'd done, the bright blue shaded leader from the south glanced up towards the heavens and said,

"Lead the way," he said, sounding much more confident than he felt.

"Stick together," ordered the new leader. "We'll flank you to make sure you're safe from any threats."

"And just what would they look like?" asked Thomas from behind, not at all keen to be surrounded in the sky by all these wicked looking dragons.

"You're not back in the land of sunshine and flowers now, my friend," urged one of their opponents. "There are many threats both in the sky and on the ground that could easily take down a dragon or two. We'll keep you safe until you get to the capital, of that you can rest assured."

"And after that?" asked the wise and experienced diplomat.

"I'm sure our leader will provide all the comfort and reassurance that you need."

Those words didn't instil confidence in any of them.

"Let's go," exclaimed For'son, bending his knees, ready to take to the sky.

Reluctantly, the others followed, each wondering what kind of threat could take down a dragon or two in the sky, and exactly what awaited them in the capital. Shortly, they would find out.

Tap, tap, tap.

"Come."

"Majesty."

"Orac. What's so urgent that you needed to see me straight away?"

"The crystals I told you about, I think I've figured out

how to make them work."

"Excellent," exclaimed the king. "When can we hope for a working prototype?"

"That's just it, I think I have one already."

"Really?"

"Yes."

"Then what are you waiting for? You have my permission to gather whatever resources you need to get it working."

There was a pause as the king, for the very first time, started to notice exactly how sheepish the rather shy and retiring librarian looked. Greger squinted, paying extra attention to the repository guardian. If Orac could have retreated into himself, he surely would have.

"What is it you're not telling me? Out with it!" demanded the king.

"I... I... I... I think I have a way of finding out what's going on in Ahrensburg, Your Highness."

"WHAT!"

Instantly the look on the librarian's face turned from awkward to afraid as the king pressed forward towards him.

"What have you done?"

"I... I... I... I secreted one of the smaller crystals on For'son before he left. I had an inkling that I might be able to get them to work quite quickly which turned out to be the case. I thought it might come in handy with the... negotiations."

Ever the pragmatist, knowing that what was done, was done, Greger considered what Orac had confessed to.

"So you're telling me we can listen in to what's happening?"

"I think we'll be able to contact For'son telepathically even across that distance, but I'll need to head up north to create a booster node first of all."

"What does that even mean?" asked the king, more than a little frustrated.

"If I can relocate some of the crystals that we brought back from China to the northern reaches of Scotland, then I think the sonic resonances will allow us to bolster the signal enough to reach our friend from here in London. Should it work, it would be confirmation that the technology could be used across the world to form a network that would create planet wide coverage. Imagine, sire, being able to contact any dragon that you wanted, anywhere in the world? How fantastic would that be?"

Nodding in agreement, Greger could clearly see the advantages, knowing more than most just how important real time communications could be to the regime that he'd set in place across most of the planet, for instance in responding to emergencies of any kind, such as natural disasters as well as possible insurgencies or rogue magic users. The potential was almost endless, he had to admit. And being able to contact his friend during the risky negotiations he was now stuck in the middle of, brought him a little comfort, knowing full well that For'son had only really agreed because of their special relationship. Getting this up and running, he decided, was of the utmost importance.

"Take whatever you need to get this done, Orac. Our full resources are at your disposal. I want to know when it's possible to safely contact For'son. Make haste."

Bowing as he left, he shouted back over his shoulder.

"Yes Majesty... I'm on it."

Watching the back of the librarian scuttle off out of the room, Greger couldn't help but wonder if he'd done the right thing, not so much sending Orac to get the crystals to work, but having sent his friend and protector to Ahrensburg. The more he thought about it, the more a nagging sense of doom chomped away at the lower part of his stomach. Trying to suppress it, telling himself, quite unsuccessfully, it was nothing, he went back to work, wondering what the hell was going on in the frosty far north.

Hemmed in all around by what remained of the diplomatic contingent that had been sent to meet them, For'son's group of dignitaries had for the most part remained silent across their group link as they soared through the skies of Ahrensburg, taking in all the unusual sights below, most of them covered in snow, ice and frost, the most unwelcoming climate and landscape for any sort of dragon, let alone those unused to the surroundings.

Brave and courageous as he was, the circumstances they all found themselves in even had For'son worried, and that was saying something. Normally optimistic, bright, forward thinking, in the past little had ever really unnerved him. But here and now he felt a chill, and not one related to the bitterly cold temperatures they found themselves battling. Something dark and insidious was in the air, of that he was sure. But what, he just couldn't put his talon on, and so out of options, and with little choice, he soldiered on, surrounded at every angle by the natives designated to bring them all to their leader. It felt very much like a chicken being delivered to the fox itself. Worried for the rest of those he was responsible for, he continued riding the nippy updrafts, pleased, at least for the time being, that his supernatural powers were deflecting the cold as they'd been designed to do. Without them, he'd be done for.

Encompassed by evil looking monstrous beasts on all sides, which wore their scars of battle with pride and anything but humility, the mood amongst the diplomats who'd been selected to accompany For'son was sombre and serious, with all of them now having some idea of just what they'd let themselves in for. If this was how it had started, what on earth would be there to greet them in the capital, they all wondered. To a being they were scared and not just a little, but were determined to do their job to the best of their ability and return home to see their families, one way or the other. Little did they know that Fate had other designs on them.

Far below, desolate frost covered plains came and went, little or no life at all visible, only long, pale green grass stretching in the harsh winds, almost always bending over backwards, the force of nature hammering home constantly. Frost encrusted lakes came and went, their flying images perfectly reflected in the thick pack ice that covered the surface, again not a single sign of life. Off in the distance, snow capped mountains rose up out of the earth, standing proud, resembling soldiers on the parade ground, respectful and quiet, some ready to erupt at any moment, noxious fiery fumes visible even at this distance. They served as a constant reminder of not only the dangers of this realm, but of just how foreign and outlandish it all was.

Although there was no chat through their telepathic link that remained constantly open at all times, it was at least briefly possible to feel another's emotions if they were left unchecked, something that the youngest of them all, Fanti, seemed to be struggling with. Not wholly unused to this situation, Thomas, the most senior of the diplomats, tried very carefully to send back a sense of reassurance and stability, encouraging the youngster to focus her mind on the tasks before her, hoping that in itself would distract her enough to get through all this.

Travelling light, with just three of the king's usual guards accompanying him, Orac touched down on one of the outlying northern isles of Scotland, three hours after his conversation with the king had ended. Fighting off the biting cold winds and the chill in the air, the librarian, having found a suitably protected environment in the form of a cave that extended back some thirty or so metres, leaving the elements well behind, opened out his bag of crystals, and selecting the most suitable surface he could see, started to use his magic to integrate the gemstones onto the side of the walls in the hope that they would maintain their integrity and serve the purpose they seemed to have been designed for.

Occasionally glancing over their shoulders at the eccentric librarian they knew the king favoured, the three hulking great dragons, one mostly yellow in colour, the next a dull, matt grey with the exception of his head that was nearly all white, the last crimson and orange, all stood back within the cave, guarding the entrance, ready for any threat, not that there should have been one, aware that the mission they'd been chosen for was important, but not understanding the details, only that they should give the librarian as much latitude as he required to get the job done. Vague didn't begin to cover the commands that they'd been issued, they all thought simultaneously, but they were as professional as they came, and very stoically got on with the mission they'd been tasked with.

Across one wall inside the grotto, Orac had lined up a series of transparent white crystals in all lengths, shapes and sizes, his supernatural power having fused them permanently in place to the dark, surrounding rock. With that completed, next he used the remaining gemstones in his pack, all various shades of purple, to line either side of the translucent ones, carefully placing each, knowing that the amplification process would depend on him getting it just right. Double checking his work, putting more pressure on himself than anyone else could, the brilliant, slightly eclectic librarian drove himself on by thinking of his friend deep within Ahrensburg, hoping that he remained safe and sound and that negotiations were going well.

Cotton wool clouds dropped from up above, obscuring their long range vision, putting For'son and his group of diplomats more on edge than they had been at any other point, the occasional glimpse of their escorts, or more like captors, as that's how it felt, sending a shiver down all of their tails and spines.

Abruptly those around and above dropped, losing altitude, forcing the diplomatic group downwards, letting the tug of gravity take them.

For a moment it was a worry until, as the clouds fizzled out, they all clapped eyes on their destination, the Ahrensburg capital, Axalangst. Set mainly against, but with some buildings up above the gigantic bluff that must have been nearly half a mile high and about five miles long, the landscape looked both alien and futuristic, with stunning water and lava falls running side by side down the solid granite cliff that separated what appeared to be an upper and lower part of the city. Three huge, clear blue rivers flanked by mighty, unfamiliar trees with warped and twisted branches meandered majestically through it all, dividing up different coloured farmland on the outer edge, the individual crops not visible at this range, but clearly nothing they were familiar with. Random flat buildings, some housing gigantic greenhouses made from extravagant panes of glass, reflected what little sunlight there was back in their direction, temporarily blinding them, that is until one of the huge fluffy clouds drifted lazily between it and the shiny surface. From where they were some twenty or so miles out, carefully arranged dwellings made from rock, slate and gigantic natural boulders, some easily three storeys high, others much lower, stretched on for miles, all radiating out from the cliff face that appeared to be not really the centre, but the height of all the activity. A huge number of dragons were flying between the upper and lower parts of the city... enormous looking metal lifts also carting an array of different goods, powered by what appeared to be geothermal energy, something those at home were only just coming to grips with. Just the sight of that made their leader think of his friend... Orac, the librarian, wondering how on earth he was getting on with his new found crystals, and whether or not he'd yet had any sort of breakthrough. It seemed unlikely given the short amount of time he'd had to study them, but For'son knew that if any dragon alive could get them to work, it would by his pal, the repository guardian, because although he didn't like to say it, the shy, retiring and eccentric dragon was one of the most intelligent beings he'd ever had the pleasure of meeting.

Plunging even lower now, resembling a plane on its final approach to the runway, high curved towers made from the same grey, granite stone as the cliff side popped up in the extended part of the enclave on the flattened ground adjacent to the sea, their curved architecture a wonder, each easily able to contain at least a dozen dragon bodies comfortably, a lookout visible at the height of their spire, appearing magnificent against the backdrop of so much water, not just the rolling waves, but the three huge rivers that appeared to flow naturally through the land.

Atop the cliff, facing out to sea, a translucent, supernatural shield ran off in the distance for as far as was visible, deflecting away the harsh weather from the upper part of the city that shone green and white, the former a thick weed-free grass in every gap where there weren't dwellings or pathways, cut to perfection, no longer than an inch tall, the latter making up the buildings, most supported by humungous pillars of shining white stone, arched rooftops, the odd sunken pool or two of crystal clear, light blue water thrown in for good measure. One gigantic lake of lava stood in the middle of it all, surrounded by the pale stone trails, none of which appeared straight, all curving around at wonderfully different angles. If gods had existed, this is where they would have chosen to live and it wouldn't have been a surprise to anybody.

Momentarily, it took the delegation's breath away, that is until their leader, the bright blue hero of the piece, pointed out exactly what was going on. "*"Look at the rising, corkscrewed spires you admire so much... tell me what you see?"* asked For'son softly, wanting them to use their brains and the information that had already been passed onto them about what they were flying into.

First to answer was the youngster, Fanti, glad to have something to take her mind off the terrible situation they all found themselves in, utterly astounded as she soared towards the fantasy setting in front of them.

"Graceful buildings, modern architecture and an abundance of food and water... it looks so calm and peaceful, and a brilliant place to live... clearly an advanced civilisation."

Across the link he could feel some of the others agreeing with not only her words but her appreciation as well. But not Thomas, no... he was far more streetwise and prepared than that.

"Look closer," urged For'son as they descended even further, curtailing some of the previous speed that they'd built up.

"Oh my..." declared Francis throughout their minds, having zoomed in on some of the more horrifying details.

One by one, the rest of them followed in Francis' footsteps, almost sick to their stomachs at their costly error. What they had mistaken for an out of the way paradise was of course nothing of the sort. The stunningly curved buildings that dotted the landscape within the confines of the city, both at sea level and atop the perfectly precise architecture of the cliff, were nothing more than guard towers, housing dragon lookouts who'd been delegated to watch over the downtrodden denizens, making sure that no laws were infringed, enforcing everything with the deadliest of magic. The more they took in, the more brutal it became with everything they'd been told beforehand all materialising before their very eyes.

Bedraggled dragons up to their knees in water worked until they dropped in the brightly coloured fields scattered precariously throughout the city, overseen by dark, hulking great monsters that enforced their cooperation by means of monstrous shadowy whips that appeared, at least from their point of view, to contain lightning itself. Occasionally one of these grisly lookouts could be seen punishing those under their watchful eye, lighting up the water all around their victims, the resulting harsh, shrill screams echoing out across the sharp, cool air. Now that they knew what to look for, dragon bodies could be seen bobbing about, face down in the knee deep water, no doubt the sick motivation to keep the other slaves in line, should they even think about escape or not giving their all.

Up in the sky, the diplomats' stomachs turned, growling and rumbling uncontrollably, their owners fighting with all they had not to regurgitate the contents of their last precious meal.

Much closer, it was now possible to see what was happening in the streets, the stand out of which was the dozen or so groups of marching emaciated dragons, all chained together via particularly dastardly metal collars that appeared to be designed to dig in and pierce the scales around their necks, thick, viscous, green blood dribbling down their torsos from the raw and open wounds. Understandably they all looked defeated and demoralised.

The high rise and low slung buildings became more apparent now, their run down states, disrepair and overcrowding obvious. This wasn't part of any paradise, more like slums of the worst kind.

And as they zipped over the outskirts, only then could they make out the festering dragon corpses swinging from the leafless tree branches all covered in rotten maggots, hung no doubt as a warning to others.

This city that looked absolutely miraculous from far away probably resembled most beings' idea of absolute purgatory. Slaves brutally beaten, killed on a whim should any form of non-adherence to the rules rear its ugly head, all living in squalor with nothing to look forward to other than pain, misery and an untimely end. As the diplomats, surrounded by their so-called guides, flew low over the conurbation, their sensitive olfactory senses were bombarded by the raw sewage flowing down some of the streets, the rotten food and fetid corpses that lay scattered haphazardly about, something that looked as though it were an everyday occurrence. To a dragon they all hoped never to encounter such evil ever again and taking everything in with their eidetic memories, vowed to redouble their efforts to bring this land back into the light and righteousness of the realm they lived in, and free these sad, enslaved beings once and for all. No one more so than For'son, who over the years had seen more than his fair share of poverty and desperation, but nothing on this scale, and that was saying quite something.

Almost as if having given them a guided tour, or quite possibly a warning as to exactly what their leader was capable of, the dark envoys, having enclosed their charges from every diffcrent angle, abruptly pulled up, taking For'son's group with them, climbing vertically up the cliff face, so close now that splashes of bright orange, searing hot magma from the lava fall peppered their scales, the sizzling warmth a welcome distraction from everything they'd just witnessed. Whistling past the edge of the cliff, the two groups tracked up a little further, levelled off and pulled a slow, lazy loop, before coming into land on a huge, lush piece of lawn adjacent to the lake of molten lava, practically in the middle of everything. Touching down with the deftness of a feather, well... the diplomats anyway, their guides not actually landing at all, only hovering a few feet above it before turning sharply and hightailing it back off over the cliff edge, all of them looked to For'son to see exactly what they should do next. With no other beings about and only the molten magma lagoon for company, the circumstances they all found themselves in was most... odd, and nothing like any diplomatic protocol he'd ever heard of. Still, they'd been guided to this exact spot for a reason, and once again, it could be another of their tests, just like his one on one battle only a short while ago, something from which he'd only just recovered. And so through the telepathic link that they all shared, he sent the shortest message he could, hoping to reassure all of them, wondering who, if anyone, could reassure him, because the longer this went on, the more uneasy he felt about the whole situation.

"Be patient," he urged. *"We wait for as long as it takes. If your mind wanders, try some meditation."*

Meditation seemed to do the trick for a few at least, including Thomas, Harold, Musim, Ecoack and Menning, lessening their worry, focusing their minds, proving a great distraction, and given what they were experiencing, was just what they needed. For the others, Francis, Radivan, S'pest, Simone and Fanti, For'son included, their environment was a challenge to say the least. Nerve wracking didn't do it justice, not knowing what they were supposed to do next, if anything at all. A few of them had wanted to go off and explore their surroundings, wondering telepathically whether that's what they were supposed to do anyway, but their brave blue leader had curtailed that straight away, stating that they'd been brought here for a reason, and that wandering around a city where they didn't belong could get them in a whole host of trouble, something they wanted to avoid at all costs. So it was that they waited, and waited, and waited some more.

"Are you finished, librarian?" one of the king's protectors asked, over the harsh wind whipping across the entrance to the cave that he found himself guarding from absolutely nothing at all.

He was, in fact he'd been finished for some time now, almost an hour, and had only been pretending to finalise a few things, because there was something that he wanted... no, needed to do, and he'd been trying to figure out the best way to go about achieving it. Having come up with absolutely nothing, and now realising the impatience of those that had accompanied him, Orac was left with little choice but to fall back on the truth... well, mostly, in his efforts to get his own way.

Standing up from a kneeling position, the squat (in dragon terms) guardian of the repository strolled purposefully over to the escorts walling off the entrance, and putting on his most sincere smile, attempted to lie his ass off.

"I'm done here," he said, all unicorns and rainbows. "It just needs testing and so I'm going to need to borrow some of your ethereal energy so that I can power the crystals and get a message back to Greger."

"What!" exclaimed the most impatient one of them, the one that had just spoken up. "The king never mentioned anything like that. We were just supposed to escort you here and make sure you stayed safe. What's going on?"

Stomach feeling like there was an out of control bowling ball bouncing around inside it, and up to his neck in it without any way back now, the librarian pressed on.

"I have strict orders from the king himself to get this working at any cost. As far as I can tell, it is, but I need to test it before we leave. And that means sending a message back to the monarch. To be able to do that, I need some of your mana to jump start the crystals into life. A little bit from each of you should do the trick."

"I'm not sure I'm too happy about that," replied one of the others grumpily, having hated every second of the miserable journey up here, the vicious winds and pelting rains of this crazy island and now the idea of this.

"Then what do you propose we do?" asked Orac angrily, now really getting into his role. "We fly back home, tell the king that we think it works, but that we couldn't test it because you wouldn't help? I can only imagine he'd get all four of us to fly straight back here, and do it all over again. Is that what you want? To let down the monarch and to be admonished by him?"

He left it hanging in the air, hoping he'd done enough... no, sure that he'd done enough, fully aware that although they might be some of the best warriors around, with the exception of his friend who was a leap and a bound above them all in that department, they certainly weren't the brightest bulbs in the box. Knowing that they were all discussing this telepathically, he waited to see just what they would decide, reasonably sure he could predict the outcome.

Nearly a minute, that's how long it took for them to make a decision.

"What is it you need us to do?"

"I just need to cast a few mantras first. After that, I need you to open yourselves up to me so that I can tap into your mana. It should be straightforward, and with all three of your sharing your gift, it shouldn't take very much out of you. After that, I'll attempt to use the crystals to boost my telepathic contact in an effort to seek out the king. It might take a while, because nothing like this has ever been done before," and, he thought only to himself, 'because that's not the first thing I'm going to do.' "After I've conversed with the monarch and gotten his approval, we can all go home."

Their relief on hearing this was almost palpable.

"Okay," continued the one in charge. "Give us the signal and we'll be ready to share."

Nodding respectfully, Orac turned and went back to checking the multicoloured gemstones, a smug smile engrained in his prehistoric face at having bested the dragons that all assumed they were superior to him. Of course they were when it came to battle and anything fighting related, but that shouldn't be all there was, should it, he thought. And so, in the darkness of the cave, over the constant howl of the wind, and with the three dragon onlookers opening themselves up to share their magic, having been persuaded to do his bidding, the librarian mouthed the final few words within his mind and, reinforced by the ethereal energy of his companions, sent his conscious will off in an effort to find his target, in totally the opposite direction to that of his king.

It felt... exhilarating, strange and utterly terrifying, his intellect branching out on its own. Okay, it wasn't his first time. On many an occasion he'd had to contact some of the clerks in another part of the capital, or one of the lookouts on the outskirts of London, but this was a different matter entirely, he thought as his psyche soared above the shadowy dark ocean, heading north instead of south, watching out for landmarks that he'd engrained into his eidetic memory so that he could do just this, in the hope of contacting his friend in an effort to make sure he was alright. Not quite instantaneously, but fast, faster than any dragon could fly, that was for sure, Orac's conscious will zoomed quicker than the speed of sound above the waves, banking a little left at the start of a mountain range, all the time on the lookout for half a dozen frozen fjords, having opted for a different route entirely to that of his friend and the party of diplomats, probably because they'd had a slightly different destination in mind, having had to rendezvous with their escorts, whereas he could head straight for the capital Axalangst, knowing that his friend For'son, should already be there by now. Worried about the little white lie he'd told to the guards in the cave with him and by omission, the king as well, the dedicated librarian soldiered on, concentrating hard on not letting his intellect wander too much, seeking out the desired landmarks, inside wondering what the capital city of this last remaining land would look like and whether or not it would live up to its foul and heinous reputation. Shortly, he would find out.

Resembling gigantic, majestic statues on the lush green lawn within distance of the bubbling and writhing lake of molten magma, For'son and his group of diplomats stood deathly still, waiting for a contact of any sort from what were supposed to be their hosts, their worry increasing with every minute that passed, nearly all of them convinced that something was very, very wrong, none more so than their leader, who, could he have gone back in time, would most certainly have done, and not have agreed to this mission in any way shape or form, and not just for his own sake, but for all of them.

With more than a hint of fear in her voice, it was Fanti who broke the shrouded silence of their minds across the joint telepathic link, startling more than a few of them, particularly those still meditating.

"I... I... I don't think they're coming. Have we done something wrong?" she asked, *"or committed some indiscretion we don't know about?"*

"If I had to hazard a guess at this point," ventured For'son, *"and that's all it is, I would suggest, very much like our first encounter, that this is some sort of test, to determine what we do, how we react or just how patient we are. Don't forget, apart from this very dubious back channel meeting that is sceptical to say the least, our two lands haven't encountered each other for over five hundred years. Much could have changed in that time, particularly the levels of paranoia. Keep still, focus your minds, eek out all the possible outcomes of what's to come, think about the potential problems and solutions... don't forget we're here to bring these beings back into the light, and given what we've seen so far, that should be our highest priority. Even if we have to wait here all night, we will, just to show our patience, attitude and the respect that we have for our hosts. From now on, keep the chat to a minimum."*

With that the link went silent, all of those with him thinking about their leader's words and how best they could distract themselves from the perilous state of affairs they found themselves caught up in.

All but doubling back on himself, Orac's mind cut through what looked like a treacherous mountain pass, lined with dark green pines, scraggy rock lines, hazardous drops and unsound build ups of snow, just waiting to drop at a moment's notice. Swallowing nervously at the danger of it all, well... back in his motionless body anyway... his intellect ploughed on regardless, knowing that he shouldn't be far away now. Hopefully once out of the mountains and across yet one more body of uncomfortably cold looking water, if he were correct, the renowned city should be directly in front of him, only a short way beyond the shoreline.

Drifting across the chilly breeze, not that he could have noticed, just before dusk, the librarian's conscious will suddenly caught sight of Ahrensburg's jewel in the crown, the capital, Axalangst. Much like his friends only a few hours earlier, he gaped in wonder at the exquisite architecture, the beautiful colours and the picture postcard scene, that is, until he got much closer. Cutting in from across the sea, he wasn't afforded quite the same view, nevertheless, the poverty, abuse and slavery were clearly evident, even from where he was. Pushing aside the sickening sight, his mind fought to regain its focus and the target it was seeking. Zipping up high in the hope of getting a better overall outlook, Orac was suddenly surprised as the previously hidden higher tier of the city swam into view on top of the cliff. He was noticing it for the first time only now, because he'd come in on a different trajectory across the harsh, dark ocean. Rising steadily, determined to take it all in, suddenly he spotted the stand out sight almost directly in the middle of it all, shining bright like a beacon in the dark. No, I'm not talking about the lake of molten lava, its orange and red contents wriggling and writhing, the steam from which rose over a mile in the air before it started to disperse. I'm talking about the instantly recognisable, blue shaded brilliant personality that stood out like someone wearing clothes on a nudist beach, his friend and the being his mind had travelled all this way for... FOR'SON!

More than a little sceptical about his whole adventure and worried that the bolstering effects of the crystals might cut out at any moment, instinctively Orac's psyche did the only thing it could in the circumstances... it altered course and, punching through the air, accelerated forward towards his buddy.

Motionless in front of the other diplomats, the hissing and popping lake of lava at their backs, the shaded blue leader of the delegation used every technique he knew to try and calm himself down and suppress the impatience within him that was starting to bubble to the surface. Abruptly, out of nowhere, his mind started to ring like a church bell on Easter Sunday.

Whether because of the crystals or the added mana from the guards back on the island at the entrance to the cave, as Orac's consciousness flew directly into his friend's mind, the only word to describe it from the librarian's point of view was... DIFFERENT! It felt as though he'd flown straight into a bog, and a muddy one at that. He was barely able to think, let alone move, now that he'd arrived at his destination. Struggling to come to terms with exactly what had happened he did the only thing he could... he called out.

"FOR'SON!" The word reverberated around his head in a voice that was strangely familiar, piercing the violent ringing that had started only a moment or so before.

"Orac?"

Attempting to find his bearings, and more importantly, shake the mental mud from his mind, suddenly his friend's dulcet tones echoed throughout all of him.

"For'son!"

For the first time in centuries the brave and mighty warrior, royal protector without equal, was knocked off his feet, caught totally unaware, well... spiritually as opposed to physically, unsure of what to make of what was going on, wary that it might be some sort of trap, given exactly where they were.

"Orac... is that really you? What's going on?"

Regaining his composure as best he could given the circumstances and the journey of a lifetime that he'd just embarked upon, oh and the fact that his mind was separated from his body by thousands of miles now, the repository guardian attempted to explain what had just happened, how he'd sneaked one of the crystals into his belly pouch before they'd departed, and how it was they could communicate with one another. To say that For'son was blown away was an understatement.

"Does the king know that you're here with me?"

A long, uncomfortable silence hung in the air, so much so that the bright blue warrior dragon almost thought that their communication had ceased through some sort of technicality... almost!

"Orac?"

Taking a long, deep breath, which of course only happened back in the cave on the Scottish Isle thousands of miles away, the librarian, torn about what to do or say, knew that he could never lie to his friend and so with that in mind, he just spat it out.

"No... he doesn't know I'm here. He thinks I'm in Scotland preparing the crystals and that my first test will be to try and contact him in London."

"Then why the hell are you here?" For'son asked, a little too angrily.

"I... I... I was worried about the negotiations, and more importantly, about... YOU!"

Now it was the warrior's turn to take a deep breath and calm himself down, knowing full well that he'd over reacted to the librarian's actions, something with hindsight he could see far more clearly now.

"I'm sorry. my friend, it was wrong of me to talk to you like that, and yes... I appreciate your actions, even if they did mean deceiving Greger."

"I just wanted to check that you were okay, that way I can report back to him that the crystals work and that negotiations are going

well. Is that what I should tell him?"

"Things haven't panned out quite as we'd hoped," For'son replied, for the first time using some actual diplomacy.

"Why are you all standing out here on your own?"

"To tell you the truth, I don't really know. We were dropped off here by what remained of our escorts and that's as far as we've got."

"What do you mean, the remainder of your escorts?"

"Oh it's no big deal, I just had to... fight one of them during our first encounter."

"And?"

"And he ended up dead."

"Oh my... that can't be good."

"It was either him or me, my friend, and I much prefer it this way round."

"I agree fully, but surely that's not normal diplomatic behaviour?"

"I think you're right, in much the same way we shouldn't be standing out here waiting for something to happen. I assume both are tests, but to determine what, who knows? Not me, that's for sure."

"Is there anything I can do to help?"

"I don't think so, not unless you can make our hosts magically appear. I think we'll have to bide our time and hope for the best. The rest of the team have severely frayed nerves at the moment, which I can't blame them for."

"I'm sorry to hear that, friend. I wish I could help."

"So do I. What are you planning to do next?"

"Currently my body's stuck on a Scottish Island guarded by three King's Guards."

That made For'son chuckle, well inside his head anyway, something of a pleasing distraction.

"I need to contact the king to let him know the crystals work in boosting telepathic range. Should I tell him about my contact with you? He'll probably be mad at me for doing so, but I don't care about that."

"Tell him, and blame me for everything, that'll take some of the heat off you. Do you think you'll be able to patch him through to me when you return to London?"

"I don't see why not. Will that help negotiations?"

"Maybe... at the very least it can do no harm. Giving him a real time update would be handy, and he'd be able to answer any big calls, should the other side ask for something that I'm simply not able to give them. I won't make them aware of what's going on, that's for sure. They'd probably never believe me anyway. I would suggest you return to your body and set about getting back to London. Tell the king everything, and don't forget... blame it all on me."

"Thanks."

"You're welcome, friend. It won't be long before I'm back, and when that happens we'll spend many a night in the library discussing everything under the sun, of that you have my word... Safe journey."

"May your negotiations be profitable and brief."

With that, the contact between the two of them was broken, the considerable mind of the librarian tearing itself away, shooting back off over the white water of the breaking waves of the shadowy sea, much faster than it had arrived, homing in on his primeval prehistoric body back in the cave on the isle, taking the most direct route possible.

Thirty seconds, that's how long it took for him to reach the inside of his own head, letting out a sigh of relief as he did so, his still form startling those that had lent him their magic for the wonderful northern adventure. Shaking off the feeling of disorientation, Orac came to his senses, shook his huge head, stomped his feet on the cold rocky floor and plodded on over to the guards, each of whom had closed themselves down on seeing him finish his experiment.

"What did the king say?" asked the most authoritative of the three.

"It didn't go as well as I'd hoped," declared the librarian, not quite a white lie, but not exactly the truth either. "We should head back to London with great haste. There are some issues that I need to discuss personally with the monarch."

Turning to his two comrades, both of whom nodded

back instantaneously to signal they were ready, all four of them bounded out of the cave and up into the cold, windswept night sky, heading south, back towards their home. Orac was pleased to have talked to his friend, alarmed at the fact that he'd had no choice but to kill one of the escorts sent out to greet them, and perplexed at them not being met in the capital. As far as he was concerned, the sooner he imparted all of this to the king in person, the better.

Blown away, despite his stoic appearance, For'son could hardly believe that Orac had broken the laws of physics as they'd known them and contacted him from so far away... what an achievement. There and then a glimmer of pride shone off him for what his pal had done. He couldn't imagine any other being across the entire planet coming up with something so outrageous, something so potentially life changing, it was absolutely remarkable. Pushing away all the farfetched thoughts about how Orac's discovery might change the world, from reacting to natural disasters, quelling mistrust and unrest to just providing help and support where and when it was needed, the diplomatic leader turned his attention back to the here and now, disappointed that they were all still standing on their own next to the fluorescent orange lake of bubbling magma that, if nothing else, was keeping them warm and toasty.

Abruptly all of them sensed movement for the very first time, off to their left from amongst a series of gigantic, matt white buildings, surrounded by huge pillars of the same colour, intricate curving paths tailing off in every direction, cutting across the perfect green lawns like a series of winding city roads. Turning their heads simultaneously, the diplomatic contingent all stood that little bit taller, ready to meet their hosts and exchange pleasantries, even after all this time kept waiting. But it was never going to be quite that straightfoward.

From out of the dark strode two humungous, battle worn dragons, chunks missing out of their thighs, massive rips visible across their wings, some of which had clearly been sewn up, but by who or what, who knew, just that it must have been a being without any skill, maybe even blind given how bad a job had been done. The dragon in the lead by a few paces had only one arm, the stump at the shoulder worn like a medal of courage, a warning to all and sundry.

Brilliant bright blue of every denomination shining bright, chest puffed out, For'son moved to stand in front of the rest of his delegation, determined to show off just how diplomatic and formal they could be, hopefully giving them a glimpse into the world that would soon become theirs.

Imagine his shock then, when the one in charge approached, all sweetness and light, and then without warning slapped him hard around the face with his remaining arm, causing his teeth to quiver and his head to buzz like a storm of bees.

'What in the...?' was all he could think, that's how much his head hurt. But there wasn't time for all that.

"Why haven't you come to find us? Are you stupid or something? I thought at the very least they would send us diplomats with at least an ounce of sense. We've been awaiting your arrival for quite some time. Our leader is not renowned for his patience. You'd better come with us now. For all your sakes, I hope he's not too pissed off."

And with that the two of them turned on their heels and stomped off into the darkness in the direction of the matt white buildings. Head pounding, cheeks flushed, full of anger and embarrassment, For'son ordered the others to follow on behind him, making it clear they were to keep their eyes peeled for even the slightest hint of treachery, no matter how unlikely or small.

Passing between two of the soft white coloured

buildings, the diplomatic contingent, lead by their enigmatic blue shaded leader entered a huge, bright white hall, the insides of which were so shiny that their reflections could be seen in nearly every surface, from the walls and ceiling, to the mirror-like floor that they strode across. Some way off in the distance, laughter and merriment could be heard, countermanding the strange, eerie silence they'd found themselves in for so long.

Following those in front, each of the dragons from the south tried their best not to look at the deathly thin dragons off to one side at different intervals, clearly there to perform menial tasks such as cleaning or waiting on those revellers up ahead. It was an all but impossible task though, their inquisitiveness winning out, forcing them to imbibe everything about the enslaved beings that were covered in bruises, and so underfed that their rib cages were visible beneath their flaking scales, something that should have been all but impossible.

For Fanti it was heartbreaking, almost to the point that she couldn't carry on, the pace of her steps slowing, out of time with the rest of them. Unnoticed by For'son because he was in front following the two dragons, one of whom had slapped him down, it was Thomas who came to her aid, telepathically anyhow, urging her to forget what she'd seen and concentrate on what was ahead, the important mission that she was a significant part of. To some degree it worked, with the young dragon falling back in time with the others, but there and then she vowed not to forget what had been done to the ordinary beings of this land and to do everything in her power to put it right, should such an opportunity arise.

As they continued to stroll purposefully along, the walls of the corridors began to become decorated with monstrous metal blades of varying sorts, from oversized scythes to swords, falcons and gigantic hammers that were still covered in sickly dried on, brilliant green dragon blood, as well as an assortment of differing shields in various states of decay. Evidently this show of power was meant to intimidate them, so on the outside they all to a being showed no signs that it had succeeded. On the inside though, that was another matter entirely, with their heartbeats going ten to the dozen, goose bumps racing up and down their spindly little arms, the pupils of their dinner plate sized eyes dilated much more than usual, all their senses heightened, each wishing they were anywhere else on the planet but here. Reaching the gargantuan oak doors from behind which the noise of the revelry originated, the two misbegotten, beaten and bruised dragons both stepped off to one side and in unison pulled open the mighty wooden gates.

If the diplomat's worst nightmares had seemingly come to pass before, things had just been ramped up to a whole new level.

A gigantic inside amphitheatre the size of fifty football pitches had been turned into a banquet hall without any equal, at least not in the grisly stakes. Amongst the roaring fires, the spit roasted meats included lamb, beef and pork, molten magma ran down the walls and across the floor, huge vats of wine and mead littered the landscape, emaciated, terrified servants waited on everyone's needs. There was sword fighting with a range of oversized weapons much the same as on the decorated corridor walls, and one on one magical contests, but a couple of things above all others stood out, immediately drawing the attention of the diplomats from the south.

Enormous dragon carcasses littered the room, scale hanging off the bone, the flesh beneath mostly torn away, some of it raw, in the hands of the revellers, a delicious pink snack to chomp on in between raucous partying, individual battles and much, much drunken merriment. Huge dragon skulls, ribs, arms feet, and talons littered the waste ridden floor. Hygiene was clearly not something any being cared about here. A stomach turning sight to be sure, one equally matched by yet one more disgusting spectacle.

In the midst of it all, upright rusted metal spits seared by the heat from the lava running down the walls, whirled around and around, the light, white meat upon them sizzling with every turn. Not so bad you might think considering everything else going on, but for two things. One, the flesh in question was human, something the diplomats were appalled at because the whole of their domain had pledged to avoid treating people as prey because they had some semblance of intelligence and a whole lot of potential, which the dragon race had recognised some time ago. And more importantly, they had been put on the spits whilst still alive, some still screaming in absolute agony as their misery continued. It was all that the diplomats could do not to throw up there and then. Fanti and a couple of others quivered in fear, their discomfort obvious to every being there, much to their delight.

No words this time, allowing only the soft reassuring touch of his presence to permeate their shared telepathic link, For'son knew that was as much as he could allow, given the circumstances in which they found themselves. He didn't doubt for a minute that something like this was a regular event, what he was sure of though, was that they'd bolstered it big time, knowing exactly how it would make them all feel. It was as though the only warm welcome these beings knew was the one that the captured humans were now currently experiencing. Bracing himself for whatever came next, he took two steps forward and stopped, the others following just behind.

Suddenly the mammoth room fell silent, all eyes focusing in on them.

From off to one side, a peppermint candy blue coloured serving dragon covered in very strange, unrecognisable white tattoos, her ribs clearly visible through her scales, bruises abounding on the left hand side of her face, approached carrying a tray full of tankards, filled to the brim with mead, currently the refreshment of the hour. Almost reaching their blue shaded leader, abruptly a dark brown beast of a monster, scars and slashes across his misbegotten face, kicked her legs out from under her, sending the tray scattering, mead splattering up the wall, her beautifully scaled head crashing into For'son's knees, the rest of her smashing clumsily into the stone floor.

"STUPID BITCH!" yelled the brown brute that had so callously instigated the whole incident, stepping forward, about to rake his talons down her thin yet stunning body in an effort to cleave her in two.

With every being there watching, all knowing exactly what had happened, predictably, honour, courage, duty and the 'right thing to do' all wrapped up in a blue form, took two steps forward placing himself in between the injured servant and the drunken reprobate, who was almost certainly acting on his leader's orders.

"OUT OF MY WAY!" he bellowed, straight into For'son's face, from about two inches away, his rancid breath washing over every part of the diplomatic leader, the stink of raw meat and offal wreaking havoc on his olfactory senses. Pushing that to one side, the southern hero and king's friend stood his ground, unflinching and resolute, readying the magic inside should it become necessary.

"Let it go!" urged Thomas through their shared telepathic link, knowing that this wasn't how diplomacy was done.

Without even an answer, For'son shrugged off the contact, choosing to ignore the envoy with the most negotiating experience of them all, instead determined to show the difference between right and wrong, good and bad, light and dark.

"STEP OUT OF THE WAY OR I'LL SLAY YOU WHERE YOU STAND, DIPLOMAT OR NOT!"

Fully centred, one foot in front of the other for perfect

balance, the shaded blue hero inhaled, and while all the time staring at his adversary, announced,

"If you think you're capable, you're very welcome to try. I might remind you though that I've already killed one of your kind today, very much against my wishes I might add. Yet one more on that tally would bother me not. Choose... and be quick about it!"

As the standoff continued, every being there held their breath, the tension in the room almost palpable, with the diplomats from the south knowing that if this went... well, you know, SOUTH, then they'd almost certainly be dead within seconds, given that there must have been at least a hundred of their opponents, probably even more, just within their line of sight.

Not one of them blinked throughout the gigantic room, all eager to see just how all this would play out. Only one being knew the answer, and that would have been the king's friend and protector, because you see, he was never going to back down, not here, not now, not... EVER! There was simply too much at stake and when I say that, I'm not talking about the negotiations or bringing the last remaining land into the dragon domain that covered the rest of the world's surface... NO! I mean he of all beings, just as he'd been brought up, trained and nurtured over the decades and centuries, would never do such a thing. Would never allow evil to rise up, show its face or the smug smile associated with its dour deeds. No longer would he play their sickening games, much like earlier, through no choice of his own, back when contact had first been made. NO! If they wanted to harm this dragon, here, now, in front of every being there, each of them well aware of exactly what had happened, then they'd do it over his dead body. A red line had been drawn, and if they wanted to cross it, he'd punish them with everything he had.

Two mighty warriors, one much more that just that, the other barely so, stood unblinking, staring directly into each other's face, both trying to get the measure of the other. Realistically though it wasn't really a contest. There only ever going to be one winner.

Blinking first in more ways than one, much to the disappointment of his leader whose gaze he attempted to attract, an angry nod was enough to get the dark brown dragon to stand down and wriggle back to his previous spot. Noting exactly what had happened, realising who was in charge at this point, For'son turned around and, keeping his senses on high alert just in case they attempted to ambush him from behind, very graciously helped the injured servant to her feet. Like the soft whisper of an artist's brush, one that only he could hear, the peppermint candy blue dragon thanked him for what he'd done but berated him at the same time for risking so much just for her. In response he just smiled, bowing his head ever so slightly as he did so.

Picking up all the dropped flagons, the servant attempted to go about her business. An outstretched hand reached out to grab her. Faster than the eye could see, even with their enhanced magical senses, For'son moved, slipping in between them, seizing the brown dragon's spindly little fingers, whilst at the same time kicking him in the shin, before spinning him around, slamming his head on the table, and holding one of the many knives in the room at his throat. Every being there readied their magic.

Tensions and lives quite literally on a knife edge, For'son glanced up directly at the being he now knew to be Nev'dir, the leader of this dastardly and cruel land, their eyes locking, neither willing to budge, both attempting to gaze into the other's soul in an effort to see what kind of being they were dealing with. For the leader of this twisted land, all he could fathom was weakness from his opponent, the kind associated with too many comforts and not enough challenges. You and I know that to be far off the mark, but that was the conclusion he quickly came to. For the leader from the south, those penetrating eyes that both resembled tortuous black holes held no end of misery and violence. There and then, he knew there was no way he could win, and would almost certainly have to go against every instinct his body held. Unfortunately... he was right!

Briefly Nev'dir smiled and that, For'son knew, was the signal. Realising an instant too late just what his leader had condemned him to, the dark brown dragon drew on all his magic in a fruitless attempt to break free. But there was no escaping the grisly fate he'd signed up for. Flooding the knife with magic to make sure it not only stayed strong, but sharp as well, all the time watching the leader who he'd come here to negotiate with, the blue shaded dragon did the only thing he could, and putting all of his power behind it, pulled the blade across the brown dragon's throat, before turning him around and slicing the whole of his front open, both acts sending bright green viscous blood spurting across the wooden tables in front of them, soaking the nearest half dozen or so patrons in the process.

Silence turned into a multitude of beings all simultaneously drawing breath, all ready to unleash their magic in an act of unmitigated revenge. However, the need to do so disappeared as their leader broke into howling laughter, just as the cadaver hit the floor at For'son's feet. Slowly, the rest of the room laughed, right on cue, all mimicking Nev'dir. It really was quite sickening.

"It would seem you have guts," chuckled the leader of this land, darkly.

"Much like your dragon here," deadpanned For'son, pointing to the recently spilled innards that lay across the filth stained floor.

"Come, all of you," announced the dragon in charge, a huge black and grey monstrosity with a crocked nose and missing molars on the left hand side of his jaw. "Join us all for a drink... I insist," he urged, motioning to some empty seats directly in front of him.

Stepping aside, For'son let Thomas lead the way, ably followed by the rest of their contingent. About to follow in their wake, suddenly a being of beauty and peppermint candy stepped directly into his path... the servant dragon who he'd stood up for only moments ago.

Appearing to be struggling with the empty flagons on her tray, subtly she leaned in, her head now close enough to speak so that only he could hear her words.

"Thank you," she whispered. "Your chivalry and courage says much about you, not least your foolhardiness."

That surprised him, but there was no time to dwell on it, because she only had a matter of moments at most.

"Take heed of what I tell you. Be careful of what you all eat and especially drink. If I had to take a guess, I'd say he's up to no good, although I have no truth on which to base that. Take care."

And with that, she side slipped around him and disappeared off through an entranceway that appeared to lead to some sort of kitchen from the look of the activity and the disgusting smells.

"COME, join us my friend," declared Nev'dir, growing impatient that For'son was the only one of the diplomatic delegation that hadn't sat down. More than a little reluctantly, the blue shaded leader did just that, positioning himself between their foul smelling leader and Thomas.

Offering out one of his grey little hands the opposition leader officially introduced himself.

"Nev'dir."

Ignoring the tinge of revolution deep within the pit of his stomach, the king's friend and diplomatic leader from the south gripped the proffered appendage.

"For'son."

"Well... For'son, you should eat, drink and be merry. In the morning we will get down to the serious negotiations. For now, enjoy the entertainment."

And that, for the time being at least, was very much

that. Music was made, alcohol in all its different forms was consumed, with everyone there but the diplomatic delegation eating heartily, the most popular dish easily the roasted humans on display. Gruesome might best describe what was playing out, but for the sake of the negotiations that they'd all been sent here for, they had to play along, at least to some degree. And so as a group for the next few hours, they did as little as they could, for the most part drinking water and eating either fruit, vegetables or in For'son's case, absolutely nothing, risking the wrath of the local leader.

Landing hard in a howling crosswind amongst a freezing shower of ice cold rain, Orac did his best to ignore the wave of pain gained from stubbing two of his talons on the rocky ground. Shooting off in front of the guards that had accompanied him on the mission, determined to reach the monarch first, he knew that he had a decision to make, one that he'd been mulling over on their treacherous flight back. What should he tell the king? The truth appeared, for him at least, the hardest option, because he knew Greger would go wild, possibly berating him, maybe even punishing him for what he'd done. But the more he thought about things, the more For'son's wise words came back, haunting him enough to make the decision for him.

Scuttling past traders plying their wares, artisans painting, carving or in some cases... spinning, the wool from the sheep reminding him of just how hungry he was, eventually the librarian reached the king's office. Without hesitation, and ignoring any of the royal protocols, wheezing like an asthmatic at the peak of a mountain, he burst in, eager to get on with things.

"Orac! What in the hell do you thi..."

"I'm sorry sire, this really can't wait," interrupted the normally timid librarian, knowing that time was of the essence.

"Did it work?" asked the king, more than a little angry at being cut short.

"In a manner of speaking," the guardian of the repository huffed, still trying to catch his breath.

"Then why are you here?"

"I... I... I... I did something... that I shouldn't have."

"And just what was that?"

"I... I contacted For'son up in Ahrensburg."

"You did what!"

"Majesty, please... let me explain."

A look of crimson red fury boiling up across his prehistoric face, it was all Greger could do not to explode.

"You were supposed to get in touch with me, not bugger about trying to contact For'son straight away. You know he's busy with the Ahrensburg negotiations and you know how much they mean. If we can pull this off, all that we've worked towards for so long will come to fruition in a relatively short time. Planet wide peace, what more of a worthy goal is there than that?"

"I'm sorry, Highness... I really am. It's just that..."

"I know, Orac. He's your friend and you wanted to make sure that he's okay, I understand, I really do. He's my friend as well, and under the circumstances, I really didn't want to have to send him, but he was the best chance to make things work, pull off a miracle like this."

"I know, sire, so does he."

"Hmmm..."

"He really does."

"And so what did he have to say in this most important of communications?"

"That he'd had to fight and kill one of the envoys almost straight away and that they'd arrived in the capital and had been kept waiting for a very long time."

Scratching at the scales around his chin, the king pondered what all of that meant... nothing good that was for sure.

"Did he say anything else?"

"Only that I should tell you the truth, sire."

"Of course, of course."

"I am truly sorry. At the very least I should have asked you."

"Yes... you should have. But that's by the by now. Can you get in touch with him again... from here?"

"I think so, yes."

"Can we both speak to him at once?"

"Maybe."

"Good... let's get on with it. What do you need?"

"I have everything here," observed the librarian, pulling a light purple crystal out from the secluded pouch that circled his belly.

Delicately placing it on the table to the side of them both, he made sure that it was securely in place before he turned to face the king.

"We need to remain undisturbed for some time. As well, I suggest we hold hands, that way there's some kind of permanent bond between us."

Nodding his understanding, the monarch strolled over to the door, opened it up and told his assistant, a tall, rather gangly dragon called Brittle, that they wished to remain undisturbed for the rest of the day on pain of death, something that shocked the wise old dragon and those around him. Shutting the door back up, Greger walked back to the table where Orac had, by now, placed two very basic wooden chairs, side by side. There was of course no hole for their tails, unlike in the dragon domain of today. It would be another ten thousand years before that became commonplace.

Reaching out to grab the monarch's hand, Greger refrained from taking it at first, wanting to ask a question.

"What's it like, interacting across a distance like that?"

"Communication is fine, clear as a bell in fact, it's tracking down the intended target that's the hard part. But don't worry, I think I can find him pretty fast having done it before. It'll be okay... it's just like flying, only faster and without all the unpleasant sensations."

"And what do I do when we finish?"

"Just think of this place, and you'll return here in a matter of seconds."

Not quite convinced, the king grabbed hold of the librarian's spindly little hand, closed his eyes, and hoped for the best.

Back in Ahrensburg the devilish debauchery and raucous revelry continued at pace, fights breaking out across the humungous indoor space, some just physical, others using magic, some of which continually missed its target, causing harm to other, innocent bystanders, although "innocent" couldn't begin to describe these warrior heathens.

As a unit, they very much kept themselves to themselves, even telepathically, only Thomas really speaking, and only then to the leader of this savage land they all found themselves trapped in, much to For'son's reluctance, although even he had to admit that Thomas knew more about all this then he ever would and so played along, quietly brooding over one of the foul beverages they'd been encouraged to drink. A sickly, chocolate brown with the consistency of treacle, it tasted worse than anything he could imagine, only managing to hold it down because Thomas had told all of them that it would be considered an insult to do anything else.

As time wore on, the partying got more out of hand, as did the personal fights, the magical battles, the outrageous bets, the bodily specific insults, the frequency and level of dares involved and of course the abuse and intimidation towards the servant dragons, some of whom had already been beaten to within an inch of their lives. And that was yet one more thing Thomas had ruled on, informing For'son that under no circumstances was he to get involved again. It was none of their business, and would be regarded as interference of the highest order, maybe even costing all of them their lives. And so, much as it didn't sit well with him, he sat there nursing his drink, occasionally speaking to one of the others in the group if spoken to first, trying very hard to ignore everything playing out around him. The only saving grace as far as he was concerned, was that the peppermint candy blue serving dragon from earlier hadn't been involved in any of it. If she had, he would no doubt have jumped in at the first sign of trouble, negotiations be damned.

'Wow!' thought the king, feeling like a dragonling again, his psyche zipping at an unerring rate over the cold dark ocean, 'Orac was right. This is just like flying, without all the sensations.' Soaking up the breathtaking sights, focusing in on the stunning white capped mountain range up ahead, back in his physical body in the capital he let out a long, slow sigh of not so much relief, as of contentment. Zooming over this magnificent scenery without the downside of the cold attacking every part of his body was almost as good as it got. Plunging down towards the shadowy sea, almost immediately they made landfall, hurtling up over the rocky beach and heading for the gap between the two nearest mountains, the king all the time able to feel the presence of the librarian beside him, almost as if they were flying in tandem. A neat trick for sure, one that he hoped would help develop the brave new world he had created, making it better for all of the beings that regarded it as their home, not just the dragon race.

Overshooting magnificent looking pine trees, unforgiving slopes, huge build-ups of sparkling soft snow, almost in the blink of an eye they rocketed out of the mountain range, across a rather treacherous looking dark lake and once more back out to sea. Still marvelling at the majestic surroundings, suddenly his private thoughts were interrupted by a familiar voice.

"We're nearly there, sire. I just thought I should let you know."

"I have to say, Orac, I'm impressed with all of this. Once this is over, you'll be richly rewarded."

"Uh... thanks, but that's not what this is all about."

"I know, my friend, I was just putting it out there though. What can we expect when we reach our destination?"

"Hopefully For'son will stand out like a beacon in the night sky. It might be though, that we have to go on a hunt for him, particularly if they're all in a building or underground somewhere."

"I'll trust you to find him and will follow your lead. Carry on."

Sweeping across yet more water, they closed in on their target, the friend that both of them were concerned about.

Speaking of which...

Clanging two gigantic iron shields together, the reverberations from which garnered every being's attention, no matter how imbibed they were, the scheming and twisted face of Nev'dir, the leader of these creatures, broke into one massive smile and started to speak.

"Listen up, the lot of you rotten scoundrels, for the time has come to toast our new found friends from the south. Staving off adversity, they've come all this way to offer us a new way of life. While I can't say I don't enjoy what we do currently, I am a strong believer in embracing change and moving with the times. And so hopefully over the coming days, we can reach an agreement that benefits both parties and brings our lands closer together. With this in mind, I propose a toast."

Right on cue, a dozen servant dragons, their heads bowed in submission, each looking frail and weak, some showing signs of a beating with bright purple, black and blue bruises littering their bodies much to the amusement of the onlookers, approached the leader and the diplomatic contingent from the south, carrying what looked like massive silver tankards filled to the brim with a thick, dark green liquid, tiny tendrils of steam and smoke rising into the air from its surface.

Slowly and very carefully, the servant dragons started to dish out the drinks to each member of the visiting negotiators. As they did so, the shared telepathic link pulsed into life.

"Uhh... is this something we should drink?" asked Fanti, more than a little nervous, her stomach already protesting just at the look of the strange concoction.

"These drinks look thoroughly disgusting," observed Menning, trying hard not to screw his face up on the outside.

"Is this wise?" asked For'son, his question directed towards the chief diplomat, Thomas, who had a whole lot more experience than him in this department, and had spent the previous hours chatting quite amicably with Nev'dir.

Thomas, a kind, honourable and decent dragon, one that garnered respect everywhere he went, had reached a crossroads in his life. Having spent nearly all his time resolving some sort of crisis, most of them violent in nature, he had little doubt that in the coming months he would be put out to pasture so to speak, probably in the form of a cushy job tucked away out of sight in the capital somewhere, diplomats per se, and him in particular, of absolutely no use once the world had been brought together. And so for him, the mission to Ahrensburg, the one he found himself in the middle of now, was something of a last hurrah, the swansong to a wonderful career, a chance to go out in a blaze of glory, his name written down in history for all to see, and know that he played a major part in finally unifying the planet. With that in mind, For'son's question about whether or not drinking what was put in front of them was wise irked him no end. Did he want to insult their hosts to the point that they would simply cancel all the talks? Was he trying to blow the deal entirely? Both of these thoughts ran through his mind as he tried to compose his answer, the need to be successful here weighing him down with as much pressure as he'd ever known. Clouded by only good intentions, one of the most loyal and honest dragons you were ever likely to meet, abruptly he did something so astounding, so out of character, that not even Fate herself could have predicted it. He... LIED! Of course he'd lied before, little white lies anyway to his children at least. But this one, this was the mother of all lies, a whopper, of that there could be no doubt. And one that would go on to cost him, the other diplomats, and the world at large, dearly.

"There's a little known mantra that the diplomatic corps uses for such occasions and I've used it to check the contents are safe to drink," Thomas said across the shared link, reassuring them all, even their blue shaded leader.

With the drinks having been served, the servants scuttling back off towards the kitchen, all trying ever so hard not to catch the eye of any of the dragon brutes there. Nev'dir continued with his speech.

"Our tradition when dealing with outsiders like this, is to finish the drink in question in one go. That way we know that you can be trusted implicitly. So," declared the vicious looking leader, "to a long lasting friendship between our two lands, and happier times ahead."

"HAPPIER TIMES AHEAD!" barked the rest of the gigantic room, all mirroring their leader and then necking their drinks in one.

With absolutely no other choice, their reasoning and decision all based on a lie, as one, For'son and the diplomats all downed their drinks in one go, ignoring the disgusting taste, slamming the tankards on the table, as the rest of the dragons had done before them. Sitting back down to much applause, little did they know, that like the human bodies all around them, their goose had very much been cooked.

Light from thousands of torches marked out the city, even from twenty or so miles away, the two minds travelling as one roared over the seashore very much like a bullet and whooshed up the cliff face, Orac closing in on For'son's last known location.

"We're here?" enquired the king, intrigued.

"Yes, sire."

"Can you see him?"

"Not at the moment, but... there!"

Even though there was no physical body, it still felt to the king like he was turning his humungous primeval head as he twisted to face the direction the librarian had indicated.

"Uh?"

"There's a faint light, one that I think connects me to his consciousness, maybe left over from last time, I'm not sure. I think we should follow it."

"Lead on."

Dropping down from the sky with the king's consciousness in tow, Orac pulled up just before he reached the perfect green lawn, something obvious even in the darkest of nights, and then corkscrewed off in the direction of two faintly lit white buildings, admiring the gigantic columns that seemed to hold them in place. Following what he'd come to think of some kind of mental tether, the pair of them, the monarch almost dragged along in the librarian's wake, slipped through huge monstrous metal doors, down an almighty corridor and into what seemed like the biggest and most raucous party in the world, absolutely appalled at what was happening before them.

And then, through the cheering crowd, they spotted all of them, finishing the last dregs of the most disgusting looking drinks they'd ever seen. Without hesitation, Orac guided them straight through For'son's head and into his cunning and well developed mind.

"FOR'SON!" bellowed the librarian, knowing that only

196

his friend would be able to hear.

"Orac! You're back. Does that mean you've returned to London?"

Before the repository guardian had a chance to answer, Greger butted in.

"It does, and we're both here this time."

"My friend."

"Indeed."

"It's great that you've returned, and how awesome is Orac getting the crystals to work, allowing us to have this conversation over such a distance?"

"He's done great work, for which I will reward him at a later date. But now, I want to know exactly what's going on here. It looks a complete and utter mess. What was it that you've just finished drinking?"

"Just some concoction that we all had to drink for a toast that Nev'dir made. Part of some long standing tradition where they welcome visitors."

"Uh... I hate to break it to you, friend," observed the librarian, *"but they have no visitors... EVER! And if they did, they'd be murdered on sight."*

"That's not what their leader said," replied For'son, feeling just a little bit out of sorts now, with two voices in his head and the commotion of the party playing out all around him.

"I don't like the sound of all this," ventured the king, starting to get extremely worried, something his friend could tell by the tone of his voice.

"It's okay," added the blue shaded diplomatic leader, *"Thomas told us all that he used the little known diplomatic mantra to check that the drinks were safe to consume, so what's the worst that can happen... we throw up just because of how disgusting it tasted?"*

If they'd been here in their physical forms, both psyches would have turned to look at each other. As it was, they couldn't, but alarm bells did start ringing within both their minds.

"FOR'SON! There's no such thing as a mantra of that kind. Of that I'm completely sure," exclaimed Greger, almost overwhelmed by panic.

"But... but... but Thomas, he told us all across our shared link. I... I... I... don't understand."

About to reassure his friend that the king was right and no mantra in existence could do such a thing, suddenly their three way conversation was interrupted by a loud crash close by, over the jeering and merriment of the crowd.

Swivelling to look at what had happened, all three were appalled to see Fanti collapsed on the filthy hard floor, thick green blood dribbling from between her jaws. Immediately For'son got to his feet, ready, willing and able to go to her aid. Or at least that was the intention. All that really happened was his head spun like an out of control fairground ride, and he collapsed back onto his huge scaly arse, holding his head firmly in his hands.

"What the...?" Orac uttered, before yet another crash got their attention, and then another and another.

Again the king and the librarian shared a look, or at least they would have, but you know what I mean.

"FOR'SON!" screamed the king, this time deep within his friend's mind, desperate to get his attention, sure that some treachery had taken place and that danger had engulfed them all.

"Uhhh..."

"FOR'SON!" yelled Orac, scared out of his... well, I was going to say mind, but given that's all there was of him there, it wasn't quite that. We'll just go with terrified beyond belief.

"Uhhh..."

"Sire?" asked the quivering librarian's consciousness.

By now the ten other members of the diplomatic delegation had all collapsed to the floor, each of them looking done for. Of course it was hard to tell for the intellect of the king and the repository guardian, not able to actually feel, hear or even smell them. But from their vantage point, which was squirreled away inside For'son's confused and confounded mind, it looked as though they all lay there either dying or dead. And just when they thought it couldn't get any worse... it did, with the confirmation they'd hoped not to have reinforced in the most gruesome and ghastly way possible.

Elegantly standing up from the seat that although not a throne in name, very much resembled one, Nev'dir used his tiny hands to signal to all those there that they should be quiet. As one they complied.

"This one," he said, motioning to For'son who remained seated, head in his hands, unable to do anything else, "should be left alone. The others, you may use as you see fit."

And as he sat down, a riot of violence and malevolence the likes of which the king and the librarian had never seen started, the crowd surging forward, grabbing individual members of the diplomatic delegation, dragging them back into their midst for their own amusement and sickening pleasure.

Too stunned to speak, not that it would have done much good because For'son seemed too far gone to recognise anything at all, let alone fight, both dragon intellects watched in absolute horror at the events taking place, teardrops running like raging waterfalls from their eyes back in the king's office in London.

Thomas was the first to be hauled out into the relative open, each of the sadistic brutes that his body passed, kicking or raking their talons down what remained of him. As the cheering became louder, roaring cones of blistering orange, yellow and red fire could just be glimpsed through what tiny gaps in the mob remained. Out of nowhere, a massive dark yellow dragon with a stump for a tail piled in, this time having procured one of the massive scythes off the wall in the corridor, the pack giving him enough room to swing it wildly, each aware of the devastation it could wreak. With a sickening THWUMP and a splatter of thick, dark green fluid, the horrific deed was done, the monster holding up Thomas' decapitated head for all to see, much to their delight.

Back in London, Orac's body started to gag, whilst Greger's empty shell trembled with rage at the futility of it all, the tears still flowing.

You would have thought that was as bad as it could get... you'd have been wrong. Systematically, the other dragon diplomats were hauled out onto the main floor, the males tortured mercilessly, some of the Ahrensburg monsters biting huge chunks of flesh and scale off their bodies, others kicking, gouging, ripping, tearing and raking their corpses apart. It was violence on a scale very rarely seen in the history of the planet. Still though, there was more.

With the librarian's consciousness having curled in on itself, far too frightened to witness any more, the king of the rest of the world, leader of dragons and one of the most decent beings on the planet forced himself to watch, knowing full well that his eidetic memory would record everything down to the finest detail. Whilst it would cause him pain and misery right up to his very end, it would at least give him something to draw upon when he dished out the orders, when he sent his army to this land to wreak vengeance for exactly what they'd just done.

Next came the females of the group, still alive but just barely, once again they were kicked, spat at and chomped on, but nothing that would end their lives too soon. Oh no, the horde had other horrors in mind for them. And I think you can probably guess what they were, over and over again, until each of them had become empty vessels, and no more use in even that department. Only after all the male dragons there had had their way were they summarily executed, in the most brutal fashion possible.

Sick to his stomach, the reigning monarch of this world, at least all of it less this one small part, continued to look on, his physical body back in London now relentlessly throwing up, not that he was aware of such a thing.

Twisted perversions satisfied, at least for now, most of the dragons left the gigantic hall, the floors covered in thick green blood, scales, organs and other unseemly bodily fluids, ready for the servants to clean up. Surrounded by a few of his most trusty lieutenants, Nev'dir spoke up, his senses and arousal heightened by what he'd just witnessed, almost ready to return to his quarters and have his way with the many concubines that his station commanded.

"What about this one?" asked an underling, spitting on For'son, hitting him on the side of his right cheek as he did so.

"Take him and string him up in the square down below in the main city. He can stay there every night. During the day he'll be paraded around. It'll be a symbol to all those who had hoped these southerners would be their salvation. Hope should be crushed and destroyed at its very first sign."

"Understood," they all replied simultaneously, standing to one side to let their leader pass.

As he trailed off, the others set about lifting the only remaining member of the diplomatic delegation still alive.

Snapped back to reality, still aware of Orac cowering somewhere close by, Greger acted as only he knew how, to save his friend.

"FOR'SON! Wake up... NOW!" he ordered, but it did little good because whatever the brew had been, it was strong that was for sure. Not killing him or even rendering him unconscious, unlike the others, he just seemed to be in a dream-like state or a trance, unable to act or bring forth his magic in any way, shape or form. Even if he could, it was difficult to see how he could escape with so many of the natives against him, making pretty much impossible odds, even for him.

"Please my friend... I'm begging you, wake up and fight your way

out of this sorry nightmare."

A strand of recognition deep within the blue shaded dragon's mind, out of nowhere suddenly realised who the voice belonged to.

"Greger," it whispered, weakly.

"For'son it's me, your friend."

"I... I... I... I've failed you, Majesty, and for that I'm deeply sorry. Your friendship has been one of the highlights of my life, I hope you know that."

"For'son... FIGHT! I command you to fight with all that you have and return home to me. YOU CAN DO THIS! DO IT NOW!"

Unfortunately he couldn't, as he was too disabled by whatever the drink had been to put up any resistance at all, and so as the other dragons started to drag him off to the different part of the city, his legs and knees scraping along the floor at odd and no doubt painful angles, his mind started to drift off into unconsciousness, which in turn meant only one thing for the squatters that currently resided there... a one way trip home!

In a flash they were tugged out of their temporary home, the city first and then the surrounding scenery of mountains, trees, snow and ice followed by rolling oceans all passing at a speed barely imaginable, even for minds like theirs, reinforced and enhanced by magic. A matter of moments later, each of them was thrust back into their physical bodies, the experience disagreeing with both of them, particularly when they discovered exactly what had happened. As well as the tears, both had thrown up on the table, Orac also peeing himself, something he was now deeply ashamed to discover in front of the king. Taking a couple of moments to come around and get their bearings, it was the librarian that spoke first.

"What... what... what can we do to get him back safely, sire?"

Rubbing his skull, trying to shake off the mother of all headaches that might have been from the experience he'd witnessed or the new found communication via the incredible crystals, only then did Greger realise that he'd never see his friend alive again. His assumption would have been correct... well, almost, but for some magic and a twist of fate. He wouldn't see him alive again, but their friendship most certainly would be rekindled.

"I think, my friend," he said turning to face Orac, "that For'son's mission will have to go down as a most selfless sacrifice. Before we'd even have a chance to get there, he'll be dead, if he isn't already. I know that's not what you want to hear, but it's a fact, and one that warrants our most voracious response. Go to your library. Take some time off, seek solace in whatever makes you happy and remember him as he would have wanted you to. He was very proud of you, you know, especially on that last mission you shared. In fact, he even talked about you going out with him on more. Coming from a dragon who liked to work alone, that's high praise indeed.

Blubbing like a lost child now, the librarian could barely take back control of his own body, let alone get a grip on it, that's how badly the grief hit him. Taking his leave, he scurried out of the office and disappeared back down to his refuge, the library, his intelligence trying to come up with anything that would help. Unfortunately for him, and in particular for For'son, nothing sprang to mind, and at least for a time, his feelings for his friend led him to spiral out of control and visit some very dark places.

For Greger though, things were different. After having shooed Orac off to his library, anger, rage, venom, fury and revenge consumed the, for the most part, mild mannered monarch, who was sick to the stomach at having been played in sending a delegation in the first place, consumed by dark thoughts at what had been done to his dragons, determined once and for all to put a stop to the evil in the north, at whatever the cost. And so it was that he summoned a council of everyone that mattered, and explained in no uncertain terms what was about to happen. And what was that, I hear you ask? One thing and one thing only... WAR!

Initially there was outrage from most of those that attended, expressing to the king in no uncertain terms that the diplomats should be allowed to do their job and continue with their mission, convinced that was the way to go. Only after slamming one of his fists down on the magnificent oak table in the council room, enhanced with enough magic to shatter it into a thousand pieces did they sit up and take notice. Really not wanting to, he persisted against his better judgement and went on to explain about the crystals and how he and Orac had sat in, so to speak, on the whole dark episode. After that, outrage soon turned into violence and vengeance, each, to a dragon, agreeing on one all out strike, the sooner the better as far as they were concerned. There and then, a mental rallying cry spread out across the lands for warriors to come forward post haste. Soon the wheels of war as was their usual wont were turning very quickly, all of their own accord.

Given his situation and what they'd done to the rest of his group last night, For'son knew he was most certainly a dead dragon walking, the time and place the only variables, his captors able to finish him off at their leisure.

And boy, were they leisurely about it. Two weeks, that's how long it took. Oh... not to kill him, but to break his indomitable will and the strength and courage that he'd shown. Two weeks might sound like a very small amount of time, but we're talking about the most vile abuse and torture, both physical and magical, his mental defences bombarded twenty four hours a day, with no let up, no break, without food or water. It was a done deal. After that, his monstrous captors paraded him around the streets in the day, chains dragging along the cobbles and hanging him up in the square at night as an example of what would happen to any invaders or challengers to the current regime. If what was done to the other diplomats was horrific, brutal and unforgiving, this was altogether on a different scale. Lesser beings would have cracked after only a few hours, and passed away after only a few more. Only his courage, bravery, loyalty and love for his friends back in the capital kept him going. But once broken, that was it. He was left an empty shell of a dragon, his huge intellect, resourceful mind, inquisitive nature, wicked sense of humour and all that was left of his personality, locked away deep inside him, in what some would regard as his soul.

The two weeks hadn't just been painful for him, with Greger having raised an army the likes of which hadn't been seen in centuries, made up of volunteers from as far away as the southern Americas. Scores of dragons attacked the barren outskirts of Ahrensburg day and night, flying deadly sorties, using magic and physicality to punish those who would stand in their way, righteousness above all on their side. Unfortunately, power, strength, ugliness and magic don't always take heed of right or wrong. And the troops under Nev'dir's command not only had nothing to lose, but were adept at using the most vicious and immoral tactics. Bait in the form of dozens of servants were laid in traps across the borders of the lands, the despicable warrior dragons of the north knowing full well that the southern softies would no doubt attempt a rescue. This played out many times over for the first couple of weeks, killing thousands of Greger's dragons, depleting their forces, making the task of taking Ahrensburg that much harder. Orac's crystals helped, laid out around the outskirts of the rebellious land, enabling those from the south to communicate and coordinate their attacks. Still though, it was a bloody battle on both sides. At one point, a squadron of those under Greger's command stumbled across a most gruesome sight, one in which they had to report back to their leader. If it wasn't for the general in charge, they probably wouldn't have realised the significance. And just what was that, I hear you ask? Decapitated dragon heads on spikes at the entrance to one of the main mountain passes, there for all to see, a message of sorts, one that stuck two fingers up in Greger's direction. You see the heads all belonged to the diplomats who had been sent to negotiate only a short time earlier, all of them there, except of course for For'son who was still alive, and still very much suffering. The general had recognised Thomas, who he'd worked with before. After that it was just a matter of communicating with the king, who managed to describe all the others to a tee. It was heartbreaking, soul destroying and had a very negative effect on morale of those from the south, not quite stopping them in their tracks, but denting their hopes and efforts considerably.

The skirmishes and battles soon became more bloody, with those under Nev'dir's command encouraged to fight until the very end, the threat of harm to their relatives, friends and loved ones suitable incentive to make them do just that. What should have been over in no longer than a month, stretched on into years, not only because of the savagery and despicable deeds carried out by those defending the north, but because of the environment, something that turned out to be as much of a problem as Nev'dir and his troops.

Much to the king and the dragon world's disgust, it took almost twenty years to take all of Ahrensburg and defeat Nev'dir, something Greger accomplished personally, in front of not only all his troops, but the remaining dragons forced into slavery in Axalangst. That was a bright day in the darkest of times which led to a new beginning not only for that land, but for the rest of the world and the beginning of peace in our time and a renaissance for dragonkind across the planet. What of For'son? He did eventually die, but it took about three months before he did so, his wicked captors constantly healing him with magic up until that point, so that they could prolong his pain and misery. But on the evening of his last living day, something extraordinary happened.

In the chill air of the frozen north, a little before sunrise, a cloaked figure skulked between the dilapidated buildings, using the shadows and dark to conceal themselves from the watchtowers and patrolling guards, avoiding the supernatural traps laid out, on a wayward path to reach their intended destination which sat smack bang in the middle of the huge cobbled square, which itself was slick with blood and adrift with cadavers, dragon and otherwise. Finally reaching a blind spot, having already crawled some way on her stomach through the gory guts and disgusting bodily matter, the slim female, shrouded in the tatty rags of what would once no doubt have been a cloak to be proud of, sprinted the rest of the way, eventually reaching her target.

Carefully she checked the chains holding the blue shaded dragon, the one who had so gallantly stepped in to save her from no doubt a very disturbing end, on his first evening in this dark and perilous land,.

'IDIOT!' she'd thought at the time, wondering why any foreigner would do such a thing. But being part of the underground resistance, she'd heard rumours of how the rest of the world lived, devoid of pain and enslavement, in absolute freedom. And so what had happened only confirmed to her what she already knew. For the rest of that first night she'd watched from a distance, hoping against hope that this wasn't another of Nev'dir's bold but stupid plans. As soon as the visitors imbibed the drinks that had been specially concocted for the occasion, she knew they were as good as dead. And that soon turned out to be the case. Like the king, she'd forced herself to watch the atrocities, much to her stomach's detriment, and was amazed to see that the one who'd saved her hadn't been instantly killed. And so after it had all ended, she'd followed and watched as best she could from a distance, as they chained him up in the middle of the square, imbuing the chains themselves with magic, stubbing out all the torches behind them so that the slaves and servants would wake up to one huge surprise and example of what not obeying the rules meant.

So here she was some months on, taking the only chance available, audaciously hoping to use what ethereal energy she had in an attempt to destroy the metal chains binding him in place, to rescue him and get the hell out of here once and for all. If she could achieve such a thing, songs would be sung in centuries to come, especially if they could return with reinforcements and free all the others. Quickly though, it became apparent that her magic lacked the sophistication to countermand that which was already there, leaving her out of options... well, all but one anyway.

Suddenly she was startled as a low, garbled grown rang out from between the frozen lips of the blue shaded prisoner.

"Please... help me," he whispered, what little breath he had left freezing in front of his face.

"I've tried to break the chains, but it's no good, I don't have either the wizardry or the power to do such a thing without setting off alarms."

Raising his head, well... as much as he could, which wasn't a great deal, he looked her straight in the eyes, recognition of their chance encounter taking a few moments.

"You!" he ventured, more in fascination than hope.

"I'm sorry for what happened," she continued, her voice barely audible. "As you can see now, our bastard of a leader is a being not to be either trusted or trifled with."

Throat too sore to speak, all he could do was nod very slightly, conveying his understanding of what she'd said.

With little else left to do and the first rays of the brilliant bright sun about to pierce the cold, dark square, time had most certainly run out for the both of them. Still though, she had one thing left to do, in return for what he'd done for her on that very first night.

"You must go, they'll spot you if you don't," he pleaded with what little strength he had left.

He was right she knew, but this had to be done, and it had to be done NOW!

Reaching up, she held one small, thin blue finger to his face, and using the ancient words that she'd been taught all that time ago, added as much of her mana as she could spare, putting all her willpower behind it. For a moment, there in the darkness, his cold, broken body glistened bright blue, before returning to its normal state. Favour returned, she leaned in and kissed him firmly on the cheek, thanked him for his bravery, before pulling the hood of her cloak back up and disappearing back into the shadows, exactly at the point that the sun's rays burst across the square, almost following her in her tracks, the brave servant dragon always just one step ahead.

As the sun bounced off the frozen cobbles of the square, temporarily blinding him, he tried in vain to wrap his mind around what the peppermint candy blue dragon from their original encounter had done to him. For certain, he felt different, but he couldn't put his finger on just how, or why. Not stronger or more powerful magic wise, he just felt as though he had a future, but that defied any logic that he tried to apply to it, because given his situation and what they'd done to the rest of his group, he was most certainly a dead dragon walking, living on borrowed time. That proved to be his very last day.

What became of him after that? His body was hung up in the square with every being told not to go near it on pain of death. Some twenty or so years later, on the day when Greger and his forces brought hope to the world, the two friends were finally reunited, and despite knowing for all those years that his friend had died, it was an emotionally charged one for not only the king, but for Orac who'd accompanied him in this one last storming of the northern capital. As the two of them nursed their dead friend's corpse in the middle of the cobbled square, every dragon there looked on, sadness and grief running riot across the lot of them. After that, what remained of For'son was taken respectfully back to London so that he could be honoured for what he'd done and endured. A fitting end for one of the planet's mightiest warriors you might think, but as some of you might already know, that's not where his story ends. Because through a twist of fate and the magic applied by the peppermint candy servant dragon, a huge part of the courageous hero lived on to not only survive, but to thrive and be reunited, for a while, with his friend the king and of course the librarian Orac, who not only recorded his friend's courage and bravery in written form for the library he loved so much, but went on to be bonded to the gorgeous Keesha and have many, many young dragonlings.

THE END

Although the end of this particular tale, if you want to find out more about For'son and his fate and whether or not he's able to help prevent the destruction of the earth some twenty thousand years later, why not check out The White Dragon Saga.

ABOUT THE AUTHOR

Paul Cude is a husband, father, field hockey player and aspiring photographer. Lost without his hockey stick, he can often be found in between writing and chauffeuring children, reading anything from comics to sci-fi, fantasy to thrillers. Too often found chained to his computer, it would be little surprise to find him, in his free time, somewhere on the Dorset coastline, chasing over rocks and sand in an effort to capture his wonderful wife and lovely kids with his camera. Paul Cude is also the author of The White Dragon Saga.

Thank you for reading...

If you could take a couple of moments to write an honest review, it would be much appreciated.

CONNECT WITH PAUL ONLINE
www.paulcude.com
Twitter: @paul_cude
Facebook: Paul Cude
Instagram: paulcude

OTHER BOOKS IN THE SERIES:
A Threat from the Past
A Chilling Revelation
A Twisted Prophecy
Earth's Custodians
A Fiery Farewell
Evil Endeavours
Frozen to the Core
A Selfless Sacrifice
Christmas in Crisis

Printed in Great Britain
by Amazon

84506614R00123